The Night House Files

CLASSIFIED

THE NIGHT HOUSE FILES

THE DEADSOUL PROJECT

Dan Smith

Illustrated by
Luke Brookes

Barrington Stoke

Published by Barrington Stoke
An imprint of HarperCollins*Publishers*
Westerhill Road, Bishopbriggs, Glasgow, G64 2QT

www.barringtonstoke.co.uk

HarperCollins*Publishers*
Macken House, 39/40 Mayor Street Upper,
Dublin 1, DO1 C9W8, Ireland

First published in 2025

Text © 2025 Dan Smith
Illustrations © 2025 Luke Brookes
Cover design © 2025 HarperCollins*Publishers* Limited

The moral right of Dan Smith and Luke Brookes to be identified
as the author and illustrator of this work has been asserted in accordance
with the Copyright, Designs and Patents Act, 1988

ISBN 978-0-00-870049-2

10 9 8 7 6 5 4 3 2 1

This book is a work of fiction. Names, characters, places and incidents are products of the writer's imagination or used fictitiously. Any resemblance to actual people, living or dead, events or locales is entirely coincidental

All rights reserved. No part of this publication may be reproduced, stored in a retrieval system, or transmitted, in whole or in any part in any form or by any means, electronic, mechanical, photocopying, recording or otherwise without the prior permission in writing of the publisher and copyright owners

A catalogue record for this book is available from the British Library

Printed and bound by CPI Group (UK) Ltd, Croydon, CR0 4YY

This book contains FSC™ certified paper and other controlled
sources to ensure responsible forest management.

For more information visit: www.harpercollins.co.uk/green

For the truth seekers

The Night House Files

Officially, the Night House does not exist. But it is real. It is an old and secret organisation that investigates the truth behind strange events around the world; events that include the paranormal, the extra-terrestrial and the bizarre. Events that governments do not want you to know about. The findings of these investigations are filed and kept safe by a mysterious person known only as the Nightwatchman. Once a year, the Nightwatchman delivers a file to me. My job is to turn the contents of the file into a story so that you can know the truth. That is the Nightwatchman's wish, and I dare not disobey.

The following story is taken from File ME347: The Deadsoul Project.

Everything you are about to read is true. The names of people and places have been altered to protect the innocent.

News article taken from the EVENING CHRONICLE, dated 8th August 2024

Alpine Heights Demolished!

Yesterday, a small crowd turned out to watch the demolition of a tower block that has long been an eyesore on the outskirts of the city.

The multi-storey building was known as Alpine Heights. It was built in 1968 to tackle a shortage of affordable housing in the city, but the building was never fully occupied. During the 1970s, some of the empty flats were used as temporary homes for soldiers awaiting family accommodation at Lightpipe Garrison army base. However, Alpine Heights was abandoned in 1977 after a health incident that resulted in a large number of deaths.

There are many local legends about the incident at Alpine Heights in 1977, but very little is known about what actually happened.

Left unoccupied since the incident, Alpine Heights fell into disrepair and decay.

Yesterday afternoon, the building was demolished in a controlled explosion and bulldozers moved in. The land will be used for the construction of luxury flats in an effort to regenerate the area.

One local who came to witness the demolition commented: "I'm glad to see the back of it. There was something wrong with that place. Something bad."

47 Years Earlier

Tuesday, 1st February 1977
6.15 p.m.

Kyle Dempsey stopped under a streetlight and looked across the deserted road at the building in front of him. *Alpine Heights*. The name made it sound like a lovely place – clean and fresh and welcoming – but it was exactly the opposite of that. Alpine Heights was a dirty grey tower stretching up into the dirty grey sky. Half the flats were empty because the mould was so bad, the bins were always overflowing and the walls were plastered with graffiti.

Oh yeah, and the lift smelled like pee.

As always, Nelson and his gang were hanging

around the entrance, under the concrete canopy, doing wheelies on their bikes.

Lauren stopped beside Kyle and kicked a stone into the long grass beside the path. A startled magpie flew up to perch on a nearby streetlamp.

"What will happen to us?" Lauren asked. Her voice was small in the icy rain. "Where will we go?"

Kyle looked down at his younger sister and sighed. "You're not going to miss this place, are you?"

"No, but ... really. Where will we go?"

"We'll be fine," Kyle said.

But right now, nothing was fine. Their whole lives had been turned upside down after they received the news on Sunday. The news about Connor.

Since then, Mam had done nothing but cry.

She was at Aunty Irene's house right now, probably still crying, so Kyle had brought Lauren home because he knew he had to get her away from that. She was only eleven, and he could see how much it was upsetting her.

Mam would be home soon enough, but for now Lauren could have some space to think about how she felt. Kyle needed some time too.

"I sort of feel bad," Lauren said. "I won't miss him. But I'm sad for Mam."

Kyle knew exactly what she meant. Mam had married Connor last year, and even though she kept telling Kyle and Lauren to call him "Dad", he wasn't their *real* dad. Their *real* dad had been killed by a hit-and-run driver the year after Lauren was born. Kyle didn't really remember him but always imagined him as kind and clever and quiet. Connor, on the other hand, was a brute who took every chance to make Kyle feel small and unimportant.

"When I was your age, I was boxing lads twice my size," he would say. Or, "What you reading a book for? You should be out causing trouble." Or there was his favourite, "Get me a drink out of the fridge, squirt."

And then there was the time in January when

Kyle and Lauren had come home from school and Mam had a black eye. She said she'd bumped it on the door, but the look on Connor's face made Kyle think it had been something else.

After that, Kyle tried to make sure Lauren was never alone with Connor Fleming.

"Come on," he said, putting an arm around his sister. "Let's go watch some telly. Maybe *The Tomorrow People* is on. I'll make hot chocolate, and there's Mini Rolls in the cupboard."

"OK." Lauren nodded and wiped the rain from her face.

As they approached the entrance to Alpine Heights, Nelson cycled over the road and started circling them on his bike. The rain flattened his spiky hair and glistened on his black leather jacket.

His tyres swished on the wet concrete path.

"All right, Soldier Boy?" Nelson said as he went round and round. "You going up?"

Nelson always called Kyle "Soldier Boy"

because Connor was in the army. He was stationed at Lightpipe Garrison just a few miles away, but there wasn't enough family housing on the base, so the army had put them in Alpine Heights until *"something becomes available"*. Connor stayed on the base during the week and came home at weekends, but last week he had been sent to Northern Ireland and would never be coming back again.

Kyle wasn't sorry he was gone, but, like Lauren, he was sad for Mam.

Nelson stopped his bike in front of Kyle and Lauren, blocking their path. He was short and stocky, with mean eyes. A padlock on a chain hung around his neck, and a skull dangled from the piercing in his left ear.

Lauren squeezed close to her brother.

"I'd normally make you pay a toll," Nelson said.

Kyle was thirteen and small for his age. Much smaller than Nelson.

"Aye," Kyle said, smiling and looking Nelson

right in the eye. "But you never charge me because we're friends, right?"

Nelson frowned. He blew a large bubble with the gum he was chewing, then looked back at his gang.

He sucked the bubble back in. "Well, I wouldn't say we're friends exactly. But I like you, Soldier Boy. You can go past."

Nelson cycled back towards the entrance.

"I said they can pass," he shouted to his gang. "It's all right."

"Come on." Kyle spoke quietly to Lauren. "Let's go."

They followed Nelson over the road and into the shelter of the concrete canopy at the front of Alpine Heights.

"I'll see you later, Soldier Boy," Nelson said.

"Aye," Kyle replied as he pushed open the heavy door and went inside. Then he and Lauren crossed the dirty lobby and pressed the button to call the lift.

When it arrived, Lauren took a deep breath and

held it all the way up to Floor 11. It was the only way to avoid the awful smell.

Escaping the lift, they trudged along the corridor to Flat 11C.

As soon as Kyle unlocked the door and stepped inside, he knew something was wrong. He wasn't sure *what*, but it made the hairs on the back of his neck stand on end.

6.27 p.m.

"Stay here," Kyle whispered to Lauren.

"What? Why?"

"Just do it," he said, reaching for the rounders bat Connor kept by the door *in case of emergencies*.

He gripped it tight and crept along the passage towards the large front room. It was mostly dark in the flat, with just a little light from the city beyond the windows, but it was enough for Kyle to see where he was going.

He eased open the door to the front room and peered inside.

Like all the other flats in Alpine Heights, 11C was small, with two bedrooms, one bathroom and one large front room. The front room was divided by a breakfast bar, separating it into a living room and a kitchen.

Right now, the living room was empty, but when Kyle looked over the breakfast bar into the kitchen, he saw a shape that shouldn't be there.

Someone was sitting at the kitchen table.

Kyle took a deep breath to steel himself.

"I've got a weapon," he said, raising the bat. "And I'm not scared to use it."

The large person didn't move and the room was in shadow, so it was impossible to tell who it was.

"I'm warning you," Kyle said. "Get out or I'll hurt you."

The person still didn't move.

Kyle edged into the living room, staring over the breakfast bar at the figure sitting in the kitchen.

With his right hand still firmly gripping the rounders bat, he stretched his left hand towards the light switch. When his fingers found the smooth plastic, Kyle flicked the switch and the room burst into light, and—

His breath caught in his chest.

Two days ago, Mam had received news that Connor Fleming had been on patrol in Belfast when a car bomb exploded right next to him. The army said it had been a massive explosion and that Connor had died instantly.

But there he was, clear as day, sitting at the kitchen table.

Kyle stood still, with the rounders bat raised above his shoulder and his mind filled with questions.

"Connor?" The word escaped his lips before he could stop it.

The person at the table slowly turned his head to look right at Kyle.

"You're ... here," Kyle said. It wasn't a question but a statement. As if by saying it out loud Kyle could convince himself that Connor actually *was* sitting at the kitchen table, dressed in his army uniform, even though he was supposed to be dead.

As reality sank in, Kyle felt a cold, creeping dread in his stomach that began to spread. Something wasn't right about Connor. He looked *wrong* – in the way the corners of his mouth lifted to form an awkward smile, and the way there was nothing in his blank, staring eyes.

When the smile didn't quite work, Connor opened his mouth, but instead of speaking, his mouth just grew wider and wider until it couldn't open any more. And he sat like that, head turned, mouth wide open, staring at Kyle.

Kyle stayed where he was, mesmerised and terrified.

"Cuh ... Connor?" Lauren's quiet voice broke the spell as she edged into the living room.

As soon as Connor saw her, his mouth snapped shut, his teeth coming together with a loud "clack". There was a brief pained expression in his eyes, then he turned to face the wall.

Lauren came to her brother's side and stared across the breakfast bar into the kitchen. "But ... I don't get it. They said he was *dead*."

Lauren whispered the word "dead" as if she didn't want Connor to hear, but Connor's head twitched once when she said it.

"Come on." Kyle took Lauren's arm and backed away without taking his eyes off Connor. He led her back along the passage into their shared bedroom.

The room was just big enough for two single beds pushed up against opposite walls, with a bedside table next to each one. Lauren's was home to a tangle of plastic jewellery and a pile of *Jackie* magazines she had found in the bin at school. She never had enough money to buy a new magazine and couldn't understand why anyone would have thrown them away. Finders keepers.

Kyle's bedside table was empty apart from a copy of *The Rats* by James Herbert. It was face-down because Lauren was scared of the picture on the front cover: a savage-looking rat with massive teeth and beady eyes.

There wasn't much else in the bedroom apart from a chest of drawers and Jasper: a raggedy pink rabbit that lay on Lauren's pillow.

Once inside the bedroom, Kyle closed the door and stood with his back to it.

"What's going on?" Lauren asked. "He's supposed to be dead, isn't he? And he looked weird. Like he was ... empty, you know?"

Kyle shook his head. "I dunno. The army must've made a mistake. Must've been someone else who died in that bomb. Or ..." Kyle stopped and rubbed his face with both hands. "I dunno."

"Maybe he's a ghost?" Lauren sat down on her bed and scooped Jasper into her arms. She hugged him as she chewed at the skin around her fingernail.

"There's no such thing," Kyle said, coming to sit down beside her. "And stop doing that."

Lauren reluctantly took her finger from her mouth, and they sat in silence for a while, both of them trying to understand what didn't seem possible. How could Connor be there in the flat when he was supposed to have been blown to pieces three days ago in Northern Ireland?

Kyle stared at the *Jaws* poster on the wall above his bed and listened to the white noise of traffic from the city outside. It was a constant sound, like the distant voices, footsteps and banging of doors that made up the soundtrack of Alpine Heights.

"We should call Mam," Lauren suggested after a while.

As she said it, the overhead light in the bedroom flickered. There was a "pop" from somewhere in the flat, like the soft and airy sound of a saggy balloon bursting.

Without a word, Kyle stood up and went to put his ear to the door.

"You hear anything?" Lauren asked, getting up.

Kyle touched a finger to his lips and shook his head. He stood for a while longer, listening, then eased the door open. He grabbed the rounders bat from its resting place against the wall and looked out.

The light was still on in the kitchen. The glow of it reached into the passageway, tempting Kyle towards it like a moth to a flame, but there was an eerie atmosphere in the flat. Something dark and dangerous. And there was a slight chemical taste to the damp air. Kyle wanted to stay exactly where he was, but he had to go out. He had to look because he had to protect Lauren. She was his little sister. His responsibility.

He crept out of the bedroom, stepping over the place where the floor creaked, and gestured at

Lauren to stay back. Lauren followed him anyway, staying close as they inched silently along the worn carpet towards the living room. As they came closer, Kyle leaned forwards to peer across the breakfast bar into the kitchen.

Everything was exactly as it had been, except for one thing.

Connor Fleming was gone.

6.47 p.m.

"Where did he go?" Lauren whispered as Kyle edged into the kitchen to check behind the breakfast bar.

"He's not here," Kyle said, returning to the living room and checking behind the long curtains either side of the window. "He must have gone out the front door."

"I didn't hear him – did *you*? And the floorboard didn't creak."

"He stepped over it then," Kyle reasoned.

"He never steps over it," Lauren reminded him.

"Well, this time he did. And then he closed the door quietly. It's the only thing that makes sense."

Lauren noticed that Kyle was still holding the rounders bat as if he was ready to hit something with it. She folded her arms around herself and shivered.

"What's that smell?" she wondered. "You smell it too, right?"

"Aye. I smell it. Like chemicals or something. Like the lab at school."

"He was a ghost," Lauren said. "That's why he's gone and that's what the smell is. It's ... ghost smell."

"Ghost smell?" Kyle scoffed. "What the hell are you talking about?" He stood by the window, wondering what to do. It was dark outside, and he could see his own reflection frowning back at him in the glass. Lauren was standing behind him, arms folded, biting her lower lip.

"We should call Mam," Kyle said, turning away

from the window and going to the little table beside the sofa where the telephone sat.

He picked up the receiver and put it to his ear, then his frown deepened. "No dial tone," he said, taking the receiver away from his ear and looking at it. "That's weird."

"There's a book in the school library about ghosts," Lauren told him. "It says they cause problems with electricity. Maybe that's what happened. The lights flickered, remember? Maybe it did something to—"

"Connor isn't a ghost," Kyle snapped at her. "There's no such thing, Lollipop. It was *him*. Connor. We both saw him."

"Don't call me Lollipop; I'm not five."

"All right. Sorry. Lauren. *Lori*." Kyle banged the telephone receiver back into the cradle and picked it up again. Still no dial tone.

Kyle slammed the telephone down again and turned to his sister. She looked small and afraid, with her skinny arms wrapped around herself. Her curls were flat from the rain, still plastered against her pale face.

Kyle took a deep breath. "Sorry. I shouldn't have got annoyed. Come on – why don't we go out?" He put his hand in his pocket and pulled out a fistful of loose change. "I've got enough for chips."

"Can we have scraps?" Lauren perked up at the thought of hot food.

"Uh-huh."

"And gravy?"

Kyle counted the coins. "Aye. For sure." He forced a smile, trying not to let Lauren see his fear, but, like her, he was creeped out. He didn't want to be in the flat one second longer than necessary.

"OK." Lauren quickly turned round and headed for the front door. "Come on then – I'm starving." She pulled it wide and waited for Kyle to catch up.

6.56 p.m.

The air in the corridor reeked of bin juice because no one ever cleaned the rubbish chutes, but Kyle didn't mind – anything was better than the weird smell inside their flat.

As he closed the door behind him, the lift clattered open further along the corridor. A severe-looking woman emerged, removing a plastic rain cover from her permed black hair. She stuffed it in her handbag and walked briskly towards them. The woman didn't live in Alpine Heights, but Kyle recognised her because she came every morning and evening to help Mrs Patel, who lived next door in 11D.

The woman's green mac left a trail of drips, and her white trainers squeaked on the tiled floor. The lift clattered shut behind her.

"Good evening," she said with a tight smile as she passed Kyle and Lauren, and went to the flat next door. She knocked hard three times, then took off her rain-speckled glasses and dried them with a handkerchief while she waited.

Kyle and Lauren had just reached the lift and pressed the button to call it back when they heard the woman knock on the door again.

Kyle looked back and caught the woman's eye.

"Excuse me," she called to him. "There doesn't seem to be any answer."

Kyle shrugged. He wasn't sure what she expected *him* to do about it.

"Mrs Patel isn't answering her door," the woman said, as if to explain herself. "Have you seen her or heard from her today?"

Kyle shook his head.

"I just thought, with you being her neighbours, you might have heard something?"

"No," Kyle replied. "Sorry."

"My name is Mrs James," she carried on. "I'm Mrs Patel's care worker. Strange that she won't answer her door. She *always* answers her door in the evening." As she spoke, Mrs James opened her handbag and rummaged inside before pulling out a set of keys. They jangled as she found the right one and slipped it into the lock. She turned it and pushed, but the door remained firmly shut.

"She must have bolted it from the inside," Mrs James said, looking back at Kyle and Lauren. "I've told her not to do that."

Just then, the lift arrived, so Kyle and Lauren stepped in and let the door shut behind them. As it closed, Kyle heard Mrs James talking to herself.

"I hope she's all right," she said.

But what she didn't know was that *nothing* in Alpine Heights was all right any more.

Nothing at all.

REPORT: X5F773-1

TOP SECRET

Interview with: JAMES DORSEY
Date: 13th March 1998

The following is taken from an interview with former Police Constable James Dorsey. This interview took place twenty-one years after the incident at Alpine Heights.

NIGHT HOUSE AGENT: As a police constable, you were first on the scene at Flat 11D Alpine Heights on 1st February 1977, is that correct?

JAMES DORSEY: Yes, it was a long time ago, but I remember it. Who could forget a thing like that?

NIGHT HOUSE AGENT: Can you talk us through what happened?

JAMES DORSEY: Well, I received a call to say that a care worker was worried about one of her patients – an elderly woman who used a wheelchair.

NIGHT HOUSE AGENT: Do you remember the woman's name?

JAMES DORSEY: Umm, the patient? Yes, she was called Mrs Patel. She lived alone in 11D and never went out, but her care worker visited every morning and evening to get her out of bed, make her a meal, that sort of thing. Well, she visited *that* evening, as usual, but became concerned when Mrs Patel didn't answer the door. Anyway, the care worker had a key to the flat, so she used it, only to discover that the door was bolted from the inside.

NIGHT HOUSE AGENT: From the *inside*? You're sure about that?

JAMES DORSEY: I'm positive.

NIGHT HOUSE AGENT: How can you be so sure?

JAMES DORSEY: Because I'm the one who broke down the door to that flat. I mean, it wasn't very strong – just a couple of good shoves and it broke, but it was definitely bolted. From the *inside*. No one could have got into that flat without breaking down the door.

NIGHT HOUSE AGENT: And did you notice anything unusual when you first went in?

JAMES DORSEY: There was a chemical smell, a bit like cleaning products. Ammonia, maybe. And something else. Sounds horrible, but it smelled like raw meat.

NIGHT HOUSE AGENT: Was there anything else unusual?

JAMES DORSEY: It's difficult to explain, but there was an atmosphere in the flat, as if something wasn't right. A gut feeling, I suppose.

NIGHT HOUSE AGENT: So then you went into the sitting room? Can you talk us through that?

JAMES DORSEY: That's what you really want to know about, isn't it? You want to know what I found. Well, I can tell you I had never seen anything like it before, and I've never seen anything like it since. What I saw in that flat still gives me the jitters, even now.

Tuesday, 1st February 1977

7.32 p.m.

Kyle only had enough money for a small portion of chips, but the woman at Marsden's Fish Shop must have felt sorry for him and Lauren. She shovelled more chips than expected onto the open newspaper and topped it off with a huge pile of scraps and a large dollop of thick gravy. When Kyle handed over his coins, the woman wiped her hands on the front of her apron and said, "Cheer up, pet – it might never happen."

Her generosity meant that the treat had lasted the whole way home, and the chips were perfect: crispy on the outside, fluffy on the inside.

They followed the path that snaked across the scruffy grass common towards Alpine Heights. The hot food and fresh air were good medicine. Kyle's mind was clear, and he felt much better with a full stomach. He had even managed to persuade Lauren that Connor wasn't a ghost.

"The army just made a mistake," he said, biting into a chip that was hot enough to burn the tip of his tongue. "He'll be there when we get back, and he'll explain everything. I'm telling you, Lori, there's an explanation for all this."

But as they neared Alpine Heights, they saw what was waiting outside the building, and a fearful cold pushed away the warmth in his stomach.

There was an ambulance by the entrance. The flickering blue lights were reflected in the cold puddles and illuminated the graffiti on the dirty concrete walls.

Nelson and his gang were there, hoods up against the drizzle, circling on their bikes like vultures. Nelson was talking to someone in the front seat of the ambulance, but when he spotted Kyle, he pushed away and cycled over the road to meet him.

"Something happening on Floor 11," he said, coming to a stop in font of Kyle and Lauren.

"Aye?" Kyle looked up at the building, squinting against the rain. There were lights on in some of the flats.

"Aye," Nelson said. "That's your floor, isn't it, Soldier Boy?"

Kyle offered Lauren the last chip, then crumpled the newspaper and threw it into the bin at the side of the path. It was a good shot.

"Apparently, someone died," Nelson said dramatically.

Kyle ignored him, taking Lauren across the road and pushing through the door into the building, where the lift was already waiting. Nelson watched them through the dirty glass, keeping his eyes on them as the lift door slid shut.

7.38 p.m.

As Kyle and Lauren stepped out of the lift onto Floor 11, two paramedics were wheeling a trolley out of the flat next door to theirs. The care worker was standing in the corridor, trembling and holding a white handkerchief to her mouth. Standing beside her was a tall uniformed policeman. Even in the poor lighting of the corridor, Kyle could see that the policeman was pale and in shock.

"Is that Mrs Patel?" Lauren whispered, staring at the trolley. There was someone lying on it beneath a pale blue blanket.

"Hold the lift!" one of the paramedics called out.

Kyle jammed his foot in the door as it began to slide shut. It thumped against his shoe, rattled, then opened.

"Cheers," said the paramedic as he and his partner guided the trolley into the lift.

Still holding the door, Kyle looked down to see that Lauren was right. It was Mrs Patel lying there with a plastic mask over her nose and mouth. She made long, slow rasping noises as she tried to suck air into her lungs. Although Kyle always thought of Mrs Patel as a large woman, she looked thin lying on the trolley.

Her face was sunken and hollow like a skeleton. Her skin was crumpled around her skull like the soggy chip paper Kyle had just thrown into the bin. And when he looked at her eyes, his heart jolted – not because they were wide open and staring dead ahead, but because they were completely, utterly black.

Kyle wanted to look away, but he couldn't. He was mesmerised by the horror of Mrs Patel's appearance.

He was nudged out of his trance only when something bumped against his leg. He looked down to see that one of Mrs Patel's hands had slipped

from under the blanket and knocked against him. Her fingers were bony and curled inwards like a claw. As Kyle stared, the fingers twitched and tried to grab the material of his trousers.

Kyle pulled away in revulsion, letting the lift door bang against the trolley.

"Careful, kid!" the paramedic said, but Kyle didn't even turn to look at him. He grabbed Lauren by the arm and walked quickly towards their front door, ignoring the policeman and the care worker.

"Did you see her?" Lauren whispered as Kyle fumbled his key into the lock and opened the door. "Was she dead?"

Kyle didn't have time to answer because as soon as they were inside the flat, Mam bustled along the short passageway towards them. She obviously hadn't been home long because she was still wearing her sheepskin coat and her boots.

"He's back," she said with a huge smile. "Connor. Your da'. He's back!"

7.41 p.m.

Mam grabbed them each by the hand and practically dragged them along the passage to the front room.

Connor was sitting at the kitchen table, just like earlier.

He was still in his army uniform, but there was more colour in his skin, and his cheeks were flushed pink under the weak yellow glow of the overhead electric light.

"The army got it wrong," Mam said as she ushered Kyle and Lauren into the living room and around the breakfast bar into the kitchen. "Your da's fine, look, and he's come home."

Connor wasn't their dad, and Kyle wished Mam would stop calling him that.

"Say hello to him," Mam said.

Mam's voice was bright with joy, but Connor didn't look up at her. He didn't even acknowledge that she was there. He just stared straight ahead with the expression of a man who didn't understand where he was or what was happening.

"Go on, say hello," Mam said again, nudging Kyle.

"Er ... hi," Kyle managed, but he had that cold, uncomfortable feeling of dread in his stomach. And it was getting worse because now that he was really looking at Connor, he could see there was something not right about him. The way he was just sitting there. The way his face was swollen and bumpy. The way the skin on his hands was rough and discoloured.

"Give your da' a hug," Mam said, pushing Lauren forwards.

"No." Lauren resisted by planting her feet firmly on the linoleum floor.

"What's wrong with you?" Mam insisted. "Give him a hug."

"I don't want to." Lauren's voice started to crack as she fought back tears.

"Just leave her," Kyle said, putting a hand on his mam's arm. "She's scared."

"Scared of what?" Mam glared at him. "There's nothing to be—"

"Stay away from me."

Connor's words were quiet and menacing.

He was staring right at Lauren with a dark and hungry look. An ugly sound rattled deep in his throat, and his pupils were so large that his eyes seemed completely black. Just like Mrs Patel's. He put his rough-skinned hands on the table as if he were going to launch himself at Lauren, but then suddenly he turned away. His chair squeaked on the floor as he twisted it, turning his back to them all. His head dropped forwards and twitched twice like he was trying to flick away an irritating insect.

"Don't look at me," Connor growled.

"What's wrong, pet?" Mam said, stepping forwards, but Kyle stopped her.

"Just leave him be," Kyle said.

Mam resisted, as if she were going to ignore Kyle, but then she relaxed and sighed deeply.

"All right," she said. "Maybe you're right. We'll leave you on your own for a bit, Connor. I'll give you some time, then I'll make some tea. Sound good?"

Mam waited for an answer, but when Connor didn't reply, she reluctantly left him in the kitchen and went into the living room with Kyle and Lauren.

"He must be tired," Mam said, brushing her blonde curls away from her face. "Something's happened to him. I've never seen him like this." She chewed the skin around her fingernail in a way that reminded Kyle of Lauren.

"You need to call someone," Kyle told her. "At the army. Find out what's going on. Why did they say he was dead?"

"Does it matter?" Mam turned on him, trying not to raise her voice. "Can't we just be glad he's here?"

Kyle sighed and looked over at Connor sitting in the kitchen with his back to them.

"There's something wrong with him," Kyle said. "Anyone can see that."

"He's just tired," Mam argued.

"It's more than that," Kyle said. "It's more like—"

"That's not Connor," Lauren whispered. "It's not him."

Mam stared down at her. She had dark circles around her eyes that were bloodshot from crying so much over the past few days. Smudged mascara streaked down her cheekbones, and her hair was a mess.

Kyle realised how exhausted she was. Suddenly, Mam looked a hundred years old.

"Of course it's him," Mam said. "Who else would it be?"

10.15 p.m.

The rest of the evening was weird. Connor didn't move from the kitchen, and when Mam cooked him a late tea of crispy pancakes with beans, he didn't touch it. Then she tried to get him to come and sit on the sofa to watch TV, but he just stayed in the kitchen with his back to them, staring at the wall.

Kyle couldn't relax, and Lauren didn't want to be anywhere near Connor, so she went to bed. When Kyle followed her an hour later, she was still awake.

"That's not Connor," she whispered to Kyle as he climbed into his cold bed on the opposite side of the room.

Kyle rubbed his feet together to get warm. He could see his breath in the air.

"It's all right," he told Lauren. "Just go to sleep. Everything will be fine in the morning."

But he didn't really believe that, and it took him a long time to fall asleep.

*

It was the early hours of the next morning, when the air was cold and the building was quiet, that an unexpected sound woke Kyle from his dark and muddled dreams.

Wednesday, 2nd February 1977
2.15 a.m.

Kyle sat up in bed, suddenly alert. He checked his watch, the dial glowing green in the dark.

Quarter past two.

He reached down for the small pocket torch he kept on the floor beside his bed. It had been a Christmas present last year. He switched it on and pointed it at Lauren's shape on the other side of the room. She was fast asleep, curled under her blankets.

The sound that had woken him came again, and Kyle flicked the torchlight up at the bedroom door.

It was closed, just as it should be, but there was

something out there in the flat, making a noise.

Kyle swallowed hard and climbed out of bed. The cold hit him immediately, and he shivered in his thin pyjamas. His breath steamed in the freezing air as he padded over to the bedroom door, listened for a moment, then opened it and slipped out into the passageway.

A faint light glowed at the end, so Kyle switched off his torch and crept past Mam's room towards the light. He was careful to step over the place in the floor that creaked. When he reached the end of the passage, he stayed close to the wall and leaned in.

Connor was in the kitchen, standing in the glow from the open fridge. At least, Kyle *thought* it was Connor. It was hard to be sure because he looked hunched, and his arms were too long. His head, too, was the wrong shape, but perhaps it was an effect of the light and shadow.

He appeared to be eating something, awkwardly holding a small tray in his oversized right hand and picking at it with the long fingers of his left hand. He was breathing heavily through his nose. In and out. In and out.

As Connor lifted those bony, claw-like fingers to his mouth, something fell from the tray and landed on the linoleum floor with a wet splat.

Connor paused as if he were going to pick up whatever he had dropped, but then he suddenly turned and looked directly at Kyle.

Kyle gasped and slowly released a breath that clouded the air in front of him.

Connor continued to stare, his black eyes glinting as his head twitched. There was something strange and misshapen about his face that Kyle couldn't make out in the semi-darkness; something hanging from around his mouth. Something that was moving.

"Stay away from me," Connor said. His voice rasped as if he were speaking through a mouthful of glass.

Then the lights in the kitchen and living room

suddenly flickered on and off with a bright flash and a strange "pop" like a wet bubble bursting.

Kyle flinched, turning his head and squeezing his eyes shut.

When he opened them again, the room had returned to darkness, apart from the soft glow from the fridge. It took a moment for his eyes to adjust, but when they did, he saw that Connor had disappeared again.

2.25 a.m.

Kyle stood looking over the breakfast bar into the kitchen, feeling confused. Where had Connor gone?

He opened his mouth to call out "Hello", as if Connor might be hiding, maybe in the cupboard under the sink, but stopped himself because what would be the point? There was no one there – he could see that. And in all the horror films he'd ever watched, people who went into dark rooms and called "Hello" were usually murdered soon after.

So he stayed quiet.

The only sounds were his breathing and the ticking of the kitchen clock.

After a long pause, Kyle crossed the threadbare orange-and-brown carpet of the living room and edged around the breakfast bar into the kitchen. The badly fitted linoleum was cold on his bare feet, but he hardly noticed because he was trying to work out what was lying on the floor in front of the open fridge door. Was that some rubbish? Could he see one corner of a polystyrene tray?

He stepped closer for a better look and felt something soft and wet squish between his toes. He jumped back, with images of squashed slugs flashing in his mind.

But there was nothing on the floor, so he leaned against the worktop and grabbed his foot in one hand. A globule of something pink and gloopy was stuck between his toes.

"Ugh," he grimaced.

How did that get there?

And as he picked it off, he had a horrific thought.

No way.

He bent down to pick up the polystyrene tray discarded on the floor. The plastic covering was torn and the contents were completely gone, except for a few remnants and some bloody liquid.

The label on the packet confirmed his worst fears: beef mince.

Connor had been standing by the fridge, eating raw mince.

REPORT: X5F773-

TOP SECRET

Interview with: JAMES DORSEY
Date: 13th March 1998

The following is taken from an interview with former Police Constable James Dorsey. This interview took place twenty-one years after the incident at Alpine Heights.

JAMES DORSEY: When I went into the flat, I found Mrs Patel in the front room, sitting in an armchair.

NIGHT HOUSE AGENT: Didn't you say she was a wheelchair user?

JAMES DORSEY: She was, but, as I understand it, she could get herself in and out of a chair, go to the toilet, that kind of thing. I couldn't see her properly because the armchair was facing the television, with its back to the door. The television was on, and the glow of it was the only light in the room. I could see Mrs Patel's arm hanging down, and I could see the side of her head, as if she had fallen asleep leaning over.

NIGHT HOUSE AGENT: So what did you do?

JAMES DORSEY: I called out to her, but she didn't respond. The television was extremely loud, and I guessed Mrs Patel was a bit deaf, so I called again, but she still didn't respond. So I went round in front of the chair, and that's when I saw what state she was in.

NIGHT HOUSE AGENT: Can you describe that for me?

JAMES DORSEY: I can try. So ... her skin was dry and papery and pulled tight around her skull. Her mouth was wide open and there were marks around it, like scratches or tiny puncture wounds. There was blood on the front of her dress, and her fingers were curled into claws. The worst thing, though, was her eyes. They were completely black. I thought she was dead, and had been for at least a few days, but the care worker told me she had seen Mrs Patel just that morning. So I went closer and took her wrist to check for a pulse. I remember how cold and light her wrist felt, and ... and then she screamed. Without any warning at all. She just started screaming. Over and over. Again and again. Seriously, it was the most horrible sound I've ever heard. I don't know how she had the energy inside her because she looked like she'd been sucked dry, but she screamed and she screamed and she screamed.

Wednesday, 2nd February 1977
7.30 a.m.

There was no sign of Connor the next morning. Mam said he must have gone to the base and insisted that Kyle and Lauren go to school as normal. They were dressed in their school uniform, ready to do as they were told, but Kyle didn't want to leave Mam alone in the flat. He tried to tell her what he had seen during the night, but Mam wasn't having any of it.

"I swear to God," Kyle insisted. "He was eating raw mince. Look." He went to the bin and took out the packet he had thrown in there last night.

Mam was standing by the breakfast bar, wearing

an old dressing gown and fluffy yellow slippers.

"Don't be daft," she said, staring into a steaming mug of tea. "Why would he eat raw mince?"

"I don't know," Kyle told her. "But he was standing right here. I saw him with my own eyes. And then the lights flickered and he was gone."

"Gone?" Mam said as the toaster popped up. "Do you know how ridiculous that sounds?"

Kyle knew *exactly* how ridiculous it sounded, and he knew *he* wouldn't have believed it if he hadn't seen it with his own eyes.

Mam put down her "World's Best Mam" mug and took the two slices of toast from the toaster. She dropped them onto a plate that she put in front of Lauren, who was sitting at the kitchen table.

"I'm telling you—" Kyle started.

"And I'm telling *you*." Mam glared at him. "I've had enough of this. Do you know what you sound like? Can you hear yourself? The army made a mistake – your da' is back and that's that. That makes much more sense than ... whatever it is *you* think. Eating raw mince? Disappearing?" She sighed and shook her head. "Really, Kyle?"

"He's not my da'," Kyle snapped. "And I don't think we should go to school today. We should stay with you and—"

"Stop." Mam cut him off. "Please. Just stop. Let me be happy, will you? Let things be normal."

Kyle took a deep breath and tried to think straight. "There's nothing normal about any of this. I mean, where is he now?"

Mam dropped two more slices of bread into the toaster. "He's gone to the base."

"Did you see him leave?" Kyle asked.

"No," Mam admitted.

"Then you don't know for sure, do you?"

"So I'll phone the base," Mam said. "Talk to someone."

"Phone doesn't work," Lauren said, scraping a thin layer of shredless marmalade onto her toast.

Mam turned on her. "Oh my God. Not you too?"

Lauren looked up from her toast and opened her mouth to object.

"Don't say a word." Mam pointed at her. "Just get your things and go to school. Now."

"Fine," Kyle said, grabbing his bag. "Come on, Lori."

Lauren hesitated, then put her half-eaten slice of toast between her teeth, snatched up the second piece and followed Kyle.

It was the last time they would ever see their mam.

4.40 p.m.

It was already dark when Kyle and Lauren walked back from the bus stop after school. It had hardly been light all day. The air was cold and damp, and the sky was heavy with dense black clouds.

Kyle hadn't been able to concentrate in lessons,

and his mates knew something was wrong when he didn't want to play football at break. They kept asking if he was all right, but he hadn't wanted to talk about it. He could tell Lauren was agitated too. She had been full of questions walking to the bus stop that morning. Why had the army said Connor was dead? Why was he acting so weird? Why wouldn't Mam listen to them? But now she was walking with her head down, not saying a word.

They were on the cracked concrete path that snaked across the scruffy common towards Alpine Heights. Broken streetlamps loomed over them, rattling in the wind. They were each lost in their own thoughts, both afraid of what they might find when they got home.

As they came closer to the building, Kyle noticed the familiar silhouettes of Nelson and his gang hanging out on their bikes.

"Hey, Soldier Boy," Nelson said as he rode out to meet them. "You're Floor 11, right?" His spiky black hair reminded Kyle of a hedgehog.

"Aye." Kyle watched Nelson circle them.

"Where that old woman got taken out yesterday?" Nelson asked, still circling.

"That's right."

"Did you see her? What did she look like?" There was a hint of excitement in Nelson's voice.

"What do you mean?" Kyle felt Lauren move closer to him.

"Did she look like she had some kind of plague?" Nelson asked.

"Plague?" Kyle repeated. "What're you talking about?"

Nelson stopped and climbed off his bike so he could push it as he walked beside Kyle. "Three more people got taken out of Alpine by ambulance today. Saw it for myself."

"Three?" Kyle looked at Nelson as he continued along the path.

"Aye," Nelson confirmed.

When they reached the entrance to the building, Nelson pointed to one of his gang – a skinny boy with bleached hair who was wearing tartan trousers and a torn denim jacket.

"That's JD," Nelson said "Floor 10. Knows a kid on his floor who found their dad lying on the sofa all shrivelled up like he'd been dead for a year, then he opened his eyes and started screaming. Freaked the kid out."

Kyle remembered what he had seen when Mrs Patel's hand had fallen from under the blanket while she was on the trolley. "Shrivelled" would have been a good description.

"And the other two were the same, from what I heard," JD said, picking his nose and wiping it on his trousers. "Both on Floor 12, all shrivelled up like school prunes. Ambulance came and took 'em away."

"Like I told you." Nelson narrowed his eyes at Kyle. "A plague."

Kyle had a sudden flash of memory from last

night: of Connor standing in the kitchen eating raw mince. There had been something strange about his face that he couldn't see in the semi-darkness. Was he like those others? Was he suffering from the same plague? Had *he* brought it to Alpine Heights?

"We have to go," Kyle said, feeling a sudden need to get inside. But as he was about to hurry away, the wail of a siren tore through the cold, dark evening.

Kyle turned to see blue flashing lights and the harsh headlamps of an approaching ambulance.

"There's another one," Nelson said. "I wonder which floor it is this time? They might as well leave an ambulance here permanently."

"Come on." Kyle nudged Lauren and hurried into the building. "We need to check on Mam."

"Good luck going in there," Nelson called after them as they pushed through the door into Alpine Heights. "Don't catch the plague!"

5.01 p.m.

Kyle had already pressed the button for Floor 11 when two uniformed paramedics – a man and a woman – wheeled a trolley across the lobby and into the lift.

"Nine, please," the woman said to Kyle.

Kyle jabbed the button with his thumb and waited for the door to close.

A moment later, the lift whirred into life and began its ascent.

"Second time today," the man muttered, taking off his cap and scratching his head. "I hope it's not like the other one."

After that, no one spoke inside the lift. The four of them stood in awkward silence until they reached Floor 9 and the paramedics whisked their trolley out into the corridor.

"This way," someone called to them. "Over here! Please, be—"

The door closed again, and the lift continued on its journey.

Kyle noticed that Lauren was picking at the skin around her fingernails so much it had started to bleed.

"It's fine." He put a hand on hers to make her stop. "Everything's going to be all right." But his mouth was dry, and his stomach was turning like a washing machine.

As soon as the lift reached Floor 11, Kyle and Lauren speed-walked along the corridor to their flat. Kyle fumbled with his key before finally unlocking the door and heading inside.

The flat was in darkness, and the sharp chemical smell was stronger than before. Kyle realised now what it reminded him of: the time Mr Andersen made them all sniff a jar of ammonia in Chemistry.

The air was even colder and damper than usual, and everything was quiet. Normally, the telly would be on, and Mam would shout "Hello, kids!", and there would be sounds drifting in from the other flats.

Life would be running its course, but right now the building seemed to be holding its breath, waiting for something. *Preparing* itself for something.

"Mam?" Kyle called as he picked up the rounders bat from beside the front door.

"Where is she?" Lauren whispered.

Kyle didn't reply. He raised the bat over his shoulder and was about to head along the passage to the front room when he heard a muffled thud.

The door to his and Lauren's room was slightly ajar, but Mam and Connor's bedroom door was firmly shut.

The noise had come from in there.

There were more sounds of movement, so he slowly approached the door. He stood in front of it, listening carefully for a long moment before he finally spoke.

"M- Mam?" His throat was dry, and the word didn't come out properly.

He knocked on the door with his free hand.

"You in there?" he asked.

There was a long pause before Mam replied. "I'm here."

"Can I come in?" Kyle turned the door handle and pushed, but the door remained firmly shut. It must have been bolted from the other side. Connor had installed the bolt a few days after they first moved into the flat. He said it was for security, but Kyle thought it was just to keep him and Lauren out.

"Not feeling well, pet." Mam's voice sounded odd. Raspy and awkward, the way Connor's voice had sounded last night. "You'd best stay away."

"What's wrong?" Kyle asked.

"I'm fine," Mam replied. "Just a bit under the weather."

"Is Connor there?" Kyle wondered. "Did you go to the base?"

"Just ... just stay away, pet, all right? Stay away from—" Mam's voice cut off as if something had stopped her.

Lauren stared at her brother in horror.

"Is it what Nelson said?" she asked. "Do they have the plague?"

REPORT: X5F7?

CLASSIFIED

TOP SECRET

Interview with: DR AYESHA CHOTRA
Date: 24th March 1998

The following is taken from an interview with Dr Ayesha Chotra. This interview took place twenty-one years after the incident at Alpine Heights.

NIGHT HOUSE AGENT: What can you tell us about the night of Tuesday, 1st February 1977?

DR CHOTRA: Well, it was a while ago, so the details are hazy, but it was an *unusual* evening, and we tend to remember things that are unusual, don't we?

NIGHT HOUSE AGENT: Perhaps if you start with Mrs Patel coming in – it was around eight o'clock, correct?

DR CHOTRA: Yes, it would have been sometime between seven and eight p.m. I was a senior doctor in the Accident and Emergency department of the Royal Charles Infirmary, and I was the first to examine Mrs Patel. She was massively dehydrated, with almost no fluids in her at all. I found an unusual injury to her neck, which was some sort of puncture wound, and her eyes were completely black. I'd never seen anything like it. But I was most concerned by the trauma she had received to her throat. It looked as if she might have swallowed something that had caused damage. Internally, I mean.

NIGHT HOUSE AGENT: What did you do?

DR CHOTRA: I sent her for an X-ray. I needed to know if there was some kind of foreign object still inside her. But there was something odd about the X-ray. It showed a dark shadow inside her chest cavity. Not her stomach; her *chest cavity*.

NIGHT HOUSE AGENT: What did that tell you?

DR CHOTRA: It didn't *tell* me anything. It *suggested* there was something inside Mrs Patel's chest cavity that shouldn't be there. I had no idea what it was, or whether it was some kind of error, so I asked for a second X-ray, which returned even stranger results. In the time between the two X-rays, no more than thirty minutes, the shadow inside Mrs Patel's chest cavity had disappeared, but her skeletal structure seemed to be undergoing some kind of change. Her ribs had thickened significantly and begun to fuse into what looked like a ... an armoured breastplate. I don't know how else to describe it. If I hadn't known better, I would have said I was looking at the X-ray of something that wasn't human.

NIGHT HOUSE AGENT: Not *human*?

DR CHOTRA: Exactly. It sounds ridiculous, doesn't it? I had no idea what I was looking at, so of course I wanted to examine Mrs Patel straight away. But when I went back to the room, Mrs Patel was gone ... and I never saw her again.

NIGHT HOUSE AGENT: What do you think happened to her?

DR CHOTRA: I don't know. But what I *do* know is that the hospital informed the police about her disappearance, and the next I heard about Mrs Patel was early the following morning as I was leaving the hospital after my shift. I was approached by two men who claimed to be from the Department of Health.

NIGHT HOUSE AGENT: But you didn't believe them?

DR CHOTRA: No, I certainly didn't.

NIGHT HOUSE AGENT: Why not? Who do you think they were?

DR CHOTRA: Military Intelligence. And before you ask, let me give you some context. My father was in Intelligence, and I met a few people in his line of work. Something I noticed about intelligence officers was that they all have a certain air about them. Especially the ones in Military Intelligence. And the people who came to the hospital that morning had that air about them. The way they dressed, the way they spoke, the words they used. And they were efficient – they took everything. Mrs Patel's medical records, her X-rays ... *everything*. And then they told me to forget I'd ever seen her. I had the impression they would have liked to wipe my memory clean of Mrs Patel, but ... well, here I am talking to you all these years later.

NIGHT HOUSE AGENT: And that's it?

DR CHOTRA: No, no. That's far from "it". You see, there were other patients from Alpine Heights that night and the following night, but then you know that, don't you? We had six in total. All of them with similar injuries, although some had a ring of puncture marks on their neck—

NIGHT HOUSE AGENT: Any idea what that was?

DR CHOTRA: Not really, but it looked as if something had fed on them, as ridiculous as that sounds. Anyway, they all had the same shadow on their X-ray, and every single one of them disappeared. The men from "the Department of Health" took their records too. They did everything they could to make it look as if those patients had never existed. The only thing they didn't do was make us sign something to keep us quiet, but then … who would believe us? They had taken all the proof.

Wednesday, 2nd February 1977
5.08 p.m.

As Kyle stood outside Mam and Connor's bedroom, dreadful thoughts threaded through his mind. First of all, there was the fact that Connor had come back from the dead. Then there was what Mrs Patel had looked like when she was taken away last night, and now Lauren had reminded him what Nelson had said about the plague. Everything was starting to piece together. Kyle was beginning to think that if there really *was* some kind of plague in the building, then maybe Connor had brought it, and maybe he had somehow given it to Mrs Patel.

And to Mam.

"Are *we* going to get it?" Lauren asked, as if she had read his mind. "The plague?"

"There *is* no plague," Kyle said without thinking. He was staring at the bedroom door, wondering whether to knock again. But before he could decide, a piercing scream cut through the air.

He and Lauren both almost jumped out of their skins.

"What the hell was *that*?" Lauren whispered into the silence that followed the scream.

"Dunno," Kyle said. "But it wasn't from here. Must have been from another flat. Someone's telly, maybe."

"That wasn't a telly." Lauren said. "That was real. That was a *person*. It—"

She was interrupted by another scream, then a loud and aggressive banging from the corridor outside.

BANG!

It was the beat of a heavy door being repeatedly slammed.

BANG! BANG!

Shaking, Lauren pressed close to her older brother as the heavy banging continued.

BANG! BANG! BANG!

"What *is* that?" Her voice was so quiet it was almost silent.

Kyle didn't answer. Instead, he inched closer to the front door and put his eye to the spy-hole.

5.10 p.m.

The view through the spy-hole was limited to a metre either side of the front door, and there was no sign of where the noise was coming from.

BANG! BANG! BANG! BANG!

The overhead lights flickered, then the banging suddenly stopped and the lights went off completely, plunging the corridor into darkness.

There was a moment of quiet, then the thump of footsteps approaching from the left. As the lights flicked back on again, a figure came into view, running fast. Kyle recognised him as the man from 11F because he had a bright red Mohawk. He sprinted past and was gone in a fraction of a second.

Then Kyle heard a heavy scritch-scratch, like a dog walking on a hard surface, and a second person came into view, moving on all fours. They came to a sudden stop right outside Kyle's front door and turned towards it.

Kyle leaned back, as if the person had looked right through the door at him. But that was impossible, right?

Tentatively, Kyle put his eye back to the spy-hole.

The figure was still there, standing on two feet now and swaying from side to side. They were wearing a light-blue hospital gown that hardly covered their misshapen body, and the exposed skin on their extended arms and legs was discoloured and rough. Their bony hands were huge, with long, clawed fingers, but it was their face that creeped out Kyle the most.

At first, he thought the person was wearing a mask because their eyes were unnaturally large, shining black orbs. But when the person twitched, Kyle realised that she was *not* wearing a mask.

And he realised something else: he was looking at what had once been Mrs Patel from next door.

As the full horror of that sank in, the lights in the corridor flickered violently, and there was a soft "pop" from outside.

When the lights came back on, Mrs Patel was gone.

A second later, there was a blur of movement from the right and the man from 11F reappeared, as if he had been thrown like a rag doll. He dropped quickly and landed on his back with a bone-crunching thump, then sat up and tried to

scramble away. But something just beyond Kyle's field of vision grabbed the man by the ankles and swiftly yanked him out of sight.

5.12 p.m.

"Jeez." Kyle backed away, still staring at the door.

"What did you see?" Lauren asked. "What's out there?"

Kyle opened his mouth and shook his head, still trying to process it all. "I ..."

"What was it?" Lauren insisted. "Tell me."

"I ... I don't know," Kyle stuttered, and the words seemed to break the spell that had fallen over him. His mind began to work once more, but slowly, like a machine still winding up to full power.

"There's something going on," he mumbled. "Something out there. We should stay in the flat."

"What do you mean?" Lauren asked. "What's out there?"

"I don't know." Kyle shook his head. "People acting crazy. I'm sure I just saw Mrs Patel from next door, except she was *running*. Like, *really running*, but on all fours like an animal. She was chasing Mohawk Guy like she wanted to kill him."

"Mohawk Guy? From 11F?"

"Aye, and she was all gnarly and twisted, like a freakin' monster. Maybe this plague is doing something to people. Turning them crazy or something."

Lauren looked up at her brother, wide-eyed and afraid. "Do you think …?" She turned towards Mam and Connor's bedroom door.

From behind it, there came a dull thud and a muffled howl of pain.

"We have to help Mam," Lauren said.

Kyle nodded. Lauren and Mam were his priority. Above everything else. He was the man of the house, and it was up to him to protect them.

Kyle backed up against the wall opposite Mam's

bedroom and took a deep breath to summon all of his strength and courage.

"OK," he said to Lauren. "Keep out of the way." And before he could lose his nerve, he threw himself, shoulder-first, at Mam's bedroom door.

The wood shuddered in its flimsy frame and there was a cracking sound, but it remained in place.

Kyle didn't waste a moment. He slammed into the door a second time, then a third and fourth. Finally, the door surround split and ripped away, flinging the door inwards so that Kyle tumbled into the bedroom.

The smell was overwhelming, and the sight that greeted him would haunt him for the rest of his short life.

REPORT: X5F809-1

T O P   S E C R E T

Interview with: PROFESSOR STEFAN ROMANO
Date: 25th November 2022

The following is taken from an interview with Professor Stefan Romano, forty-five years after the incident at Alpine Heights.

Professor Stefan Romano was one of the lead scientists on **Project TP731**. The project came to the attention of the Night House many years after the events that occurred at Alpine Heights in February 1977. Until then, there had been no explanation for what happened. It took agents many years to identify the twelve scientists who worked on **Project TP731** and to find one of them who was willing to be interviewed.

Two weeks after this interview, Professor Stefan Romano disappeared. His whereabouts are still unknown.

PROF. ROMANO: No one can know I have spoken to you. This interview *must* be kept secret, do you understand? This wasn't a minor experiment; this was something *world-changing*. I know they're still watching me, even after all this time.

NIGHT HOUSE AGENT: But you think it's important to tell us the truth, Professor Romano. You said you want people to know about Project TP731. That's what we're here for.

PROF. ROMANO: Yes. Yes, of course, I did, didn't I? So what can I tell you? Well, I can tell you that the aim of Project TP731 was to investigate the possibility and applications of teleportation.

NIGHT HOUSE AGENT: *Teleportation?* You're talking about making something disappear in one place and reappear in another? Instant travel?

PROF. ROMANO: Well, it's incredibly more complicated than that, but yes, that's about it. It has always been possible in *theory*, but in *secret*, things had progressed. We made teleportation a reality. We were teleporting living beings from here to there in an instant.

NIGHT HOUSE AGENT: Can you explain how that works?

PROF. ROMANO: It would be like explaining quantum theory to a chimpanzee. No offence.

NIGHT HOUSE AGENT: None taken. Perhaps you could explain in simple terms?

PROF. ROMANO: Very well. In simple terms, we had a Teleportation "Send" Chamber and a Teleportation "Receive" Chamber. The subject entered the Send Chamber, and when the system was activated, the subject was deconstructed – broken into billions of particles – and reconstructed almost instantly in the Receive Chamber. Understand?

NIGHT HOUSE AGENT: I think so. You're saying the subject was transported from one chamber to another, instantly.

PROF. ROMANO: Quite so. To begin with, we tested it on mice, then we progressed to monkeys. At first, the tests were a failure. The animals were not reconstructed properly. They were inside out, or had limbs in the wrong place, or their eyes were missing, that kind of thing. It was very messy.

NIGHT HOUSE AGENT: But you continued with the experiments?

PROF. ROMANO: Of course. We recalibrated the machines, learned from our mistakes and kept trying until the subjects came through successfully. Or that's what we thought. They looked healthy, and everything was in the right place, but there was something missing. Something we couldn't see. It wasn't so obvious with the mice, but the monkeys' behaviour was different. One of the researchers said it was as if the flesh had been teleported but not the soul. That's when some of the junior scientists on the team began calling it the Deadsoul Project.

NIGHT HOUSE AGENT: Did you identify the problem?

PROF. ROMANO: We didn't have time. It was a military project, and the generals wanted results. All they saw was the successful teleportation of living subjects. They were excited about the possibilities and wanted us to test it with human beings, so they sent us one. His name was Private Connor Fleming.

NIGHT HOUSE AGENT: Why him?

PROF. ROMANO: Why not? I imagine his name was chosen at random because he was no one. He didn't matter.

NIGHT HOUSE AGENT: Did Connor Fleming know what was happening?

PROF. ROMANO: He was told the machine was a health scanner, so he went in without complaint.

NIGHT HOUSE AGENT: You didn't think that was wrong?

PROF. ROMANO: It's not my job to decide what's right and what's wrong. I'm a scientist. I deal with facts. Possibilities and impossibilities.

Private Connor Fleming was the test subject, so that was that. We fired up the Send Chamber, and he disappeared. He was broken down into billions of tiny particles, just as expected. But unexpectedly, he didn't reappear in the Receive Chamber.

NIGHT HOUSE AGENT: So what happened to him?

PROF. ROMANO: All I know for a fact is that Private Connor Fleming went into the Send Chamber and disappeared. I have no idea what happened to him after that. The army made up a cover story about a bomb in Northern Ireland, and his wife was informed.

NIGHT HOUSE AGENT: But you do know something, don't you? Because Connor Fleming reappeared two days later, in his home, where he was found by Kyle and Lauren Dempsey, his stepchildren.

PROF. ROMANO: Apparently so.

NIGHT HOUSE AGENT: Do you have an explanation for that?

PROF. ROMANO: No.

NIGHT HOUSE AGENT: You have no idea where Private Fleming had been?

PROF. ROMANO: Well ... I have no way of testing this theory, but there must have been something different about teleporting a human. Something more complicated. Perhaps he passed through a different reality ... a different world ... a different *universe*. There's so much we don't know.

NIGHT HOUSE AGENT: And why do you think he reappeared at his home?

PROF. ROMANO: Again, I'm guessing, but I think it was a place that meant something to him. Perhaps if I'd had the chance to examine him ... The only thing I know for certain is that Private Fleming was not the same when he reappeared. Wherever he went, whatever happened to him, he *changed*. Maybe there was a little bit of him left at first, a part of him that didn't want to hurt those children, because apparently he told them to stay away from him. But that part wasn't there for long. And after that, when he changed completely, well, then he wasn't Private Fleming any more, was he? He was something else.

Wednesday, 2nd February 1977

5.16 p.m.

The door smashed inwards, and Kyle fell into his mam's bedroom. When he stuck out his hands to stop himself falling flat on his face, they sank into a damp, papery gunk covering the floor. It felt gross on his skin, and he quickly scrambled backwards onto his knees. He sat there, trying to get his bearings.

Mam's bedroom was bigger than it should have been. The far wall was gone, and the soft, damp gunk Kyle had fallen into stretched right through into the flat next door, smothering the carpet and walls. It was a layered grey mass that reminded Kyle of the wasp nest he had seen last summer behind the temporary classroom at school.

There were pieces of broken furniture sticking out from the grey mass close to where Kyle had fallen – a chair leg, the corner of a bedside table, the end of a chest of drawers. The wardrobe that once stood against the near wall was now lying on its side with large pieces torn out of it. It looked like it had been chewed up and spat out to build the weird papery dome that filled the space where Mam's bed should have been.

Kyle was convinced he was looking at a nest, but that wasn't the worst of it.

There were bodies lying in the semi-darkness, half covered in shining, snotty gunk. They were pale and thin, with eyes as black as ink. Their mouths were open in silent screams.

Mrs Patel was standing at the entrance to the nest. At least, Kyle thought it was Mrs Patel, but she hardly looked human any more. Tatters of her

pale-blue hospital gown had fused into her lumpy, leathery skin. Her waist was narrow, her chest was wide and she was hunched over, standing on legs that had grown an extra joint and clawed feet. She had long, twisted arms with large, clawed hands that held on tight to Mohawk Guy from 11F. He was limp in her grip, and his skin was shrivelled like an old orange.

Beyond her, the silhouettes of four or five other creatures moved about in the grey mass. Some looked mostly human, but others were more like Mrs Patel, with hunched backs and extra joints in their limbs. They were busying about on all fours, rearranging the grey material as if enlarging the nest.

It was almost too much for Kyle to process – it was *too* different, *too* alien. He felt a sudden and almost overwhelming need to laugh. He had to bite down on his tongue to stop himself as he shuffled backwards, hoping the creature that had once been Mrs Patel hadn't noticed him burst into the room.

But she was too distracted. She was holding

the man with the Mohawk as if she was waiting for something to happen.

And then something *did* happen.

A pair of long, leathery limbs unfolded from the entrance to the nest, followed by the most monstrous thing Kyle had ever laid eyes on.

The creature was bigger than a human, but it was hunched over and moved on four legs, as if it were still getting used to its own body. Spiny hairs sprouted from the top of its head, and bulbous eyes glinted like orbs of black glass. Its mouth was surrounded by long, fleshy, saw-toothed tentacles that moved with a life of their own. There were patches of army uniform fused into its skin, and Kyle knew that this thing – this *horror* – emerging from its nest was Connor Fleming.

Or what was left of him.

The creature twitched its head and clambered across the papery grey mass towards Mrs Patel.

"No."

It was Lauren who said it, and it was just one word, but it was enough to break the spell that held Kyle in place.

Behind him, in the passage, Lauren was backed against the wall, watching in terror.

Kyle got to his feet and went to her. He put a hand over her mouth as the Connor-thing crawled fully from its nest and went to accept the gift Mrs Patel was offering. When Connor was close enough, the tentacles around his mouth darted forwards and clamped onto Mohawk Guy's face. Then a long, snake-like tongue darted out from Connor's mouth. With a wet choking sound, it slithered into Mohawk Guy's open mouth and down his throat.

Kyle didn't want to see any more. He didn't want to watch Connor feed on Mohawk Guy, so he pulled Lauren towards the front door.

"We have to get out of here," he said.

"What about Mam?" Lauren asked.

"She's gone," Kyle told her. "Mam is gone."

5.18 p.m.

Kyle opened the front door and cautiously checked the coast was clear. They had to get away from the flat.

"OK, come on." He stepped out into the corridor, but Lauren stayed where she was.

"We have to get Mam," she said.

"I told you – she's gone." Kyle hated saying it.

"But—"

Kyle tightened his grip on Lauren's arm.

"You saw what I saw," he hissed. "If she was in that room, she's gone. I have to look after *you* now. I can't let anything happen to you." He pulled her out into the corridor and closed the door behind them. "Come on."

Lauren hesitated, resisting her brother as she stared at the dark bloodstain on the floor close to their front door.

"Is that where it got him?" Lauren asked. "Is that where it got Mohawk Guy?"

"Aye, maybe," Kyle muttered, but he ignored the blood and scanned the corridor as they headed closer to the lift.

"What *are* those things?" she asked. "Was that *Connor*?"

"I think so."

A long scream echoed somewhere far off in the building, followed by a series of shouts and heavy bangs.

Kyle stopped and listened.

"They killed Mam," Lauren said. "Didn't they? Connor killed her."

"Try not to think about it," Kyle told her. "We need to concentrate on getting out of here. We'll get to the lift and—"

"But what if it's everywhere? Like all over the building, I mean. What if *everyone* is one of those things now?"

"They're not," Kyle said.

"How do you know?" Lauren sounded empty.

Numb. "And what if this plague is, like, *everywhere*? Even outside."

"It isn't," Kyle insisted.

They were close to the lift now, just a few more paces, but then the lights in the corridor flashed bright, and there was a soft, wet "pop" from behind them.

Kyle and Lauren spun round to see Connor standing a few metres further down the corridor.

The light was brighter now, so they had a better look at him in all his horror. His hunched back and his brown leathery skin. His crooked legs and his extended arms with gnarly claws where there should have been hands. The tentacles around his mouth writhed and coiled, their jagged edges rubbing together to make an eerie scratching sound.

"Oh flip," Lauren muttered under her breath.

As she said it, the lights flickered again, plunging the corridor into complete darkness. Then, a fraction of a second later, the lights flashed back on again.

Connor was right in front of them now. Somehow, he had covered the distance between them in less than a heartbeat. He grabbed Lauren in his claws and lifted her up so that her feet dangled several centimetres above the ground. The tentacles on his face reached out to clamp on to her as his snake-like tongue slithered from his small, fleshy mouth.

"Kyle!" Lauren screamed. "Help!"

Kyle reacted by raising the rounders bat and bringing it down on the creature's head as hard as he could.

The wood thumped against Connor's face and deflected downwards to strike the tongue that was extending from his mouth.

Connor reacted instantly, releasing his grip on Lauren and letting out an ear-splitting screech.

Lauren fell to the floor and picked herself up quickly as the corridor filled with a chorus of popping sounds and the lights flickered violently.

"Oh my God," Kyle said as the lights settled. "There's more of them."

Several creatures had appeared a couple of metres behind Connor. One was wearing the remains of a suit, his jacket stretched wide, the shirt burst open to reveal his leathery chest. A ripped tie dangled around his neck. A woman in orange pyjamas stood beside a man in a tracksuit. All were in different stages of mutation. And there, standing closest to Connor, was a twisted creature with pieces of a hospital gown fused into her skin.

Mrs Patel.

Except she wasn't Mrs Patel any more. Like Connor, she now had large, shining black eyes of the darkest jet. And instead of tentacles, she had large lips around a circular mouth that was filled with tiny, vicious teeth.

Kyle didn't waste any time. He raised the rounders bat and hit Connor as hard as he could. This time, Connor screeched and went down, giving Kyle and Lauren the chance to run.

There was no time to wait for the lift, so they sprinted past it and slammed through the door into the stairwell. Side by side, they raced down the first flight of stairs just as the lights began to flicker.

"They're coming!" Lauren yelled.

Creatures popped into the stairwell behind them, but Kyle and Lauren kept going, leaving the creatures behind. They skidded past the door to Floor 10 and continued down past 9, 8, 7, 6, but when they reached Floor 5 and turned the corner to head down the next flight of stairs, they came to a sudden stop.

The stairwell was blocked by a creature that already had a young man in its grip. Its lips were clamped on to his neck, and it made weird sucking noises as if it were feeding on him. The sound turned Kyle's stomach, but it only lasted a few seconds. Then the lights flickered, there was a "pop", and both the creature and the man were gone.

"What the hell?" Lauren muttered as the lights flickered again and another creature appeared at the bottom of the stairs. It twitched its head as it looked up at them, then it let out an ear-shredding screech and scuttled towards them on all fours.

REPORT: X5F809-

TOP SECRET

Interview with: PROFESSOR STEFAN ROMANO
Date: 25th November 2022

The following is taken from an interview with Professor Stefan Romano, one of the lead scientists on **Project TP731**, forty-five years after the incident at Alpine Heights.

NIGHT HOUSE AGENT: Did you ever see any of the victims from the Alpine Heights incident?

PROF. ROMANO: Our team examined a few, but only briefly. All the bodies, all the specimens and all of our research was quickly confiscated and taken away from us. Most of the victims we *did* see had a circular puncture wound to their neck, which explained how the creatures fed.

They latched on with sharp teeth and sucked fluid from their victims, much like a lamprey would. You can look that up if you don't know what a lamprey is. It's a jawless eel-like creature sometimes called a "vampire fish" that—

NIGHT HOUSE AGENT: We know what a lamprey is, Professor Romano.

PROF. ROMANO: Oh. Right. Well, anyway, the feeding didn't kill the victim. Instead, it appeared as if something had then attached to the victim's face and reached down inside them, through the mouth, to implant a thick tar-like mass that could've been some kind of DNA. *Whatever* it was, it grew inside them and caused the transformation. But I didn't examine any creature with the ability to do that.

NIGHT HOUSE AGENT: They couldn't *all* do it?

PROF. ROMANO: No. None of the specimens we saw could have implanted anything into the victims. They could only feed.

NIGHT HOUSE AGENT: So how do you think it happened?

PROF. ROMANO: The only explanation is that there was something I didn't see. A "queen" or "king" creature that implanted the mass into the victims. I imagine it as something like a queen bee at the centre of a hive, creating more and more workers who would bring it more and more victims.

NIGHT HOUSE AGENT: Could Connor Fleming have been the "king"?

PROF. ROMANO: That would be my theory. I believe that Mrs Patel was his first victim, followed by a handful of others. Some of them were taken to the local hospital, but they didn't stay there for long. You see, I believe Connor Fleming had fed on them and implanted something that grew inside them. Something that *changed* them into some kind of "worker". Those workers then returned to him, like worker bees returning to their queen, to assist in the nest-building and to hunt. I believe their job was to deliver him more victims, which he could turn into more workers, and so on. Magnificent, really, when you think about it. The creature doesn't actually kill anyone; it just feeds on them, then turns them, creating an army of workers.

NIGHT HOUSE AGENT: How long did the mutation take?

PROF. ROMANO: A matter of hours, as far as I can tell. That's why the number of creatures grew so rapidly. It was estimated that Connor

Fleming infected five or six people on his first night in the building. Now, just imagine if each of those brought him five or six more victims to infect. And each of those brought five or six victims, and so on. The numbers grew rapidly. And many of those victims lived alone, so no one knew they had been infected.

NIGHT HOUSE AGENT: And what about their ability to appear and disappear at will?

PROF. ROMANO: All my research was taken away and supposedly destroyed, so I can only guess but ... well, I think it was an effect of the original experiment. In simple terms, those creatures were teleporting. You mentioned that the police had to break down Mrs Patel's door because it was bolted from the inside?

NIGHT HOUSE AGENT: That's correct.

PROF. ROMANO: Well, bolted doors don't stop creatures that can teleport. But I'm only guessing. Project TP731 has been shut down and all the evidence has been "destroyed". Officially, anyway.

NIGHT HOUSE AGENT: Do you think the project has continued "unofficially"?

PROF. ROMANO: I'm convinced of it. The lab was closed and all the equipment was taken away, but to where? I'd bet my life the lab has been built elsewhere. Think about it … why would the military simply stop such a project? How could they ignore technology like that? Just imagine a military that is capable of teleportation, or a military with the ability to infect a population the way Alpine Heights was infected. No, no, that technology is still being tested, I'm sure of it. In fact, I have even heard that Private

Connor Fleming was successfully retrieved from the building.

NIGHT HOUSE AGENT: Alive, you mean? You're suggesting that Connor Fleming was taken from the building *alive*?

PROF. ROMANO: Oh yes. Very much alive. I imagine he'd make a very interesting test subject, don't you?

Wednesday, 2nd February 1977
5.23 p.m.

The creature scuttled up the stairs towards Kyle and Lauren. It moved on all fours, its claws rasping on the filthy concrete steps. As it came, the lights flickered again, followed by an airy popping sound as another creature appeared in the stairwell behind it.

"This way!" Lauren shoulder-barged through the door onto Floor 5.

Kyle followed, the two of them bursting into the corridor, hoping to find safety, but Floor 5 was in chaos. Doors were banging, and people were screaming. Residents were rushing towards them, and creatures were appearing in the flickering light behind them.

A panicking young woman shoved past, escaping into the stairwell straight into the arms of the advancing creatures. The closing door muffled her shrieks. Halfway along the corridor, two men were sprinting towards them, one of them yelling at Kyle to hold the door. Before he could shout again, a creature appeared in front of him, wrapped its arms around him and bit down on his neck. The second man didn't even pause, but as he passed the lift, long arms reached out, swiped him off his feet and dragged him inside. There followed a loud scream and frantic banging against the metal interior of the lift.

Kyle looked around, frantically searching for an escape. They couldn't run back into the stairwell, and it would be suicide to head along the corridor. But then Kyle spotted an open door to one of the flats just a few metres to his left, where the corridor was clear. Lauren saw it too, and she looked at her brother. They nodded to each other, then made a run for it.

Lauren went in first, then Kyle eased the door closed behind them, careful not to make a sound. He kept his fingers curled around the handle as they both stopped and listened.

The horror continued out in the corridor for a minute or two before, finally, an eerie silence descended.

"Safe?" Lauren dared utter only a single word.

Kyle narrowed his eyes and listened.

Eventually, he nodded but kept the rounders bat ready to strike as they crept into the living room. There was no sign of anyone – or any*thing*.

"Empty," he whispered. He breathed out a long sigh and sat on the arm of the sofa. His whole body was trembling, and he needed to rest.

Lauren sat beside her brother, and the two of them remained quiet for what felt like a long time.

"I'm scared," Lauren whispered eventually.

"Me too," Kyle told her.

"But we'll be OK, right? We'll get out of here."

"Aye," Kyle agreed.

"How though?" Lauren asked. "*How* do we get out of here? It's too high to climb down. There's only the stairs or the lift."

"We wait for things to get quieter," Kyle said. "Then we go and look – see if the coast is clear."

"Do you think anyone is coming to help?" Lauren wondered.

"Definitely," Kyle replied, trying to sound hopeful. "We probably won't even have to sneak out. Someone will come – the police probably, or the army – and we'll be rescued."

"Unless those things are already out there," Lauren said quietly. "Out in the world, I mean."

Kyle tried not to imagine the horror of those things out in the world, spreading everywhere.

"What even are they?" Lauren looked at her brother.

"Dunno." Kyle shook his head. "But did you see the way they just appeared?"

"And there's that weird popping noise like they're pushing the air out of the way – or it's rushing in to fill the empty space when they disappear. Do you think they're some kind of alien? Like in *Doctor Who*?"

"They're people," Kyle said. "At least, they *were* people. Something happened to them. Like a disease or something. I mean, that was definitely Mrs Patel from next door, wasn't it? And I recognised the kid from down the corridor."

"And Connor," Lauren said. "That was him. The one you hit."

"Aye, it was. And it looked like he was in charge. Did you see the way they all came to help him when I hit him? It actually felt pretty good, you know?" Kyle said. "Hitting Connor."

Lauren looked at her brother and smiled despite everything that was happening. Kyle let himself smile back at her, and a huge ache filled his heart.

"I won't let anything happen to you," he said. "I swear."

"I know," Lauren replied. "And I won't let anything happen to you." She stood up and moved quietly towards the kitchen area.

The flat was the same design as their own, with a breakfast bar instead of a wall between the kitchen and living room, so Kyle could see Lauren open a drawer.

She pulled out a large wooden rolling pin and held it up for Kyle to see.

"Now I have a weapon," Lauren said grimly, then turned when something caught her eye.

"What's wrong?" Kyle asked, jumping to his feet and readying his bat.

At first, Lauren didn't reply. She turned and went to the end of the kitchen, looking through a long, rain-spotted window across the city in front of Alpine Heights.

"Flip," she said, putting her face close to the glass and looking down. "Check this out."

"What?" Kyle was already moving to join her at the window. "What is it?"

5.31 p.m.

Fifteen metres below, the concrete area at the front of Alpine Heights was a hive of activity. An ambulance and two police cars lay abandoned, with their doors wide open. Behind them, several olive-green Land Rovers were parked bumper to bumper. Armed soldiers stood guard by the Land Rovers.

Five large military trucks had driven up onto the grass either side of the path, and soldiers swarmed out from the back of them. Some soldiers set up plastic barriers to surround the building. Others took up guard positions or moved electric floodlights into place.

"Flippin' heck," Lauren muttered. She narrowed her eyes against the sudden brightness of a floodlight pointed directly at the building.

"It's the army," Kyle said. "They're here to rescue us."

As he said it, three black vans appeared along the road and screeched to a halt. The back doors flew open, and soldiers jumped out carrying automatic weapons. Dressed entirely in black, they had hoods pulled over their heads, and their faces were covered by gas masks. They jogged towards the barrier, ducked under and stopped behind the line of Land Rovers. They paused for a moment, then moved around the vehicles and slowly approached the entrance to Alpine Heights, splitting into four tight groups.

"Special Forces," Kyle said. "Those things don't stand a chance now. We're going to be OK."

"Wait," Lauren whispered, pressing closer to the glass to look down. "Something's happening."

The four groups of soldiers in black had stopped and dropped to a crouch. Their weapons were raised and pointed forwards. The faint sound of shouting drifted up to the flat.

A second later, two people appeared from the front of the building.

The soldiers in black were coiled like snakes ready to strike as they started to inch forwards, still shouting orders. The two people from the building continued to approach, and there was more shouting followed by a staccato rattle of gunshots.

The two people collapsed onto the concrete. One of the groups of soldiers hurried forwards to check the bodies, while another group jogged into the building. The other two groups followed, and within moments they were out of sight.

"Oh my God." Lauren put a hand to her mouth and looked at her brother in horror.

"They shot them," Kyle whispered. "They ... do you think those people were infected or just trying to get out? I mean ... they wouldn't just shoot people, would they?"

"What if they think *we're* infected?" Lauren said. "What if they shoot *us*?"

Before Kyle could answer, the lights in the flat flickered and there was a soft "pop" a few metres away in the living room.

They both knew what it meant.

5.33 p.m.

Kyle ducked behind the breakfast bar and pulled Lauren with him. They crouched there, staring at each other, listening to the creature's raspy breathing from the living room just a few metres away.

White light from the floodlights outside illuminated the room with an eerie glow.

Kyle's mouth was dry, and his heart was thudding in his chest. He was sure it was loud enough for the creature to hear, but it didn't seem to be moving. Not yet.

Kyle held a hand up to his sister, palm open.

Don't move.

Lauren nodded once.

There was a scuffing noise as the creature took a step. Then came the chilling sound of its teeth clicking together.

Kyle rose up until his eyes were just above the breakfast bar.

The creature was there, in the middle of the living room, with its back to him. It stood still, twitching its head from side to side, clicking its teeth together and taking another step.

It was searching the flat.

Kyle lowered himself behind the breakfast bar and turned to Lauren. He pointed at himself, then at her, then towards the way out of the kitchen.

You and me. We're getting out.

Lauren widened her eyes and shook her head.

No way.

Kyle nodded.

Yes way. We have to.

The creature was looking for them. It would search the flat, and eventually it would find them. The only option was to leave now, while it had its back to them.

Kyle scowled at Lauren and beckoned with one hand before turning away and crawling along the kitchen floor. When he reached the end of the breakfast bar, he stopped and raised a finger to his lips.

Stay quiet.

Then he rose again to look over the breakfast bar.

The creature was on the other side of the living room, beside the sofa. There was nowhere else in the room for it to search. Any moment now, it would turn and come towards the kitchen.

It was now or never.

Kyle ducked down and looked at Lauren, then pointed to the way out.

Now.

Lauren nodded.

All they had to do was make it to the living-room door, along the passage and out into the corridor. It was a journey that would take seconds on an ordinary day. A journey that Kyle would make without even thinking – could probably do with his eyes closed. But right now, it felt like a journey of a thousand miles.

He summoned all his courage and got to his feet. He stayed low as he crept around the end of the breakfast bar and into the living room.

The creature was still there, at the far end, with its back to him.

They were going to make it. If they could get out before it turned around, they would be fine.

Lauren stayed close to her brother as they edged further into the living room.

The door into the passage was just four steps away now.

Kyle kept his eyes on the monster.

Three more steps. That was all.

The creature twitched its head, listening.

Two more steps

Its teeth chattered.

Kyle paused, his concentration shifting from the creature to the door and back again. He was almost there, but the creature twitched again, as if it were going to turn.

It was now or never.

Kyle took two quick steps towards the living-room door and into the passage.

But then he made a mistake.

The rounders bat in his right hand knocked against the doorframe.

It wasn't a loud noise. Just a tap, really. But it was enough.

The creature spun round and saw them

immediately. In an instant, it popped out of existence and reappeared in the passage right in front of Kyle. It reached out with long arms to snatch him up.

5.36 p.m.

Kyle was quick. He stepped back, swiping his rounders bat at the creature's claws. He struck it hard, making it bellow a high-pitched screech of pain. Thick spittle sprayed from its mouth, spattering Kyle's face and burning his skin. He threw up his hands to protect himself and stumbled into Lauren, who was standing behind him. Lauren lost her balance, and the two of them tripped over each other, falling backwards into the living room.

The creature scuttled forwards like a giant cockroach and crouched over Kyle. It grabbed his shoulders with incredible strength as it pushed him hard to the ground.

Kyle found himself lying on the grubby carpet

face to face with the creature. His nostrils filled with the awful smell of chemicals and raw meat as he looked up into its shining black eyes. It was like looking into the eyes of a giant, soulless insect, and Kyle saw his own reflection in those black orbs. He saw the fear in his own eyes as the creature leaned towards his neck and opened its mouth wide.

Kyle looked right into that fleshy mouth filled with rows of vicious teeth and knew this was the end for him. There was no way to escape.

But as the creature prepared to feed, it suddenly twitched as if something had disturbed it, then Lauren appeared over its left shoulder. She held the rolling pin, one hand at each end, and reached over the creature's head to pull it back hard into its mouth. Immediately, the creature's teeth clamped down on the wooden rolling pin, and it reared upwards. Lauren held tight and pulled back hard as she swung up onto the creature's back.

Kyle took the chance to scramble into the living

room and jump to his feet. In the passage, Lauren continued to torment the creature. She clung to its back, her arms either side of its head as she held the rolling pin tight in its mouth. For one crazy second, it looked as if she were riding it like a horse.

Like that, the creature stumbled into the living room, spinning about and screeching.

Kyle grabbed the rounders bat from where he had dropped it and rushed forwards to attack. He didn't care where he hit it; he just struck again and again, beating the twisting, spitting monster as it struggled to throw Lauren from its back.

Lauren held tight as the creature crashed into a lamp stand, making it topple over. The lamp's bulb exploded against a wooden side table. An armchair overturned with a thump, and Kyle's rounders bat smashed into a glass coffee table that shattered into a thousand shards.

Finally, when the creature stumbled against the upturned armchair, it leaned forwards and lowered its head, giving Kyle the opportunity to end the fight once and for all.

He lifted the rounders bat over his shoulder and twisted his hips, preparing to hit it harder than he had ever hit anything before. And at just the right moment, he released his swing.

It was a good shot. Hard enough to have cracked a coconut.

But there was a "pop", and the creature disappeared.

The bat swung through thin air, only just missing Lauren as she dropped to the carpet. Kyle spun round from the force of his own swing, smacking the bat hard against the wall. It punched through the plasterboard, and a shockwave vibrated up his arms.

It felt as if the fight should have been over, but the creature wasn't giving up. It popped back into existence by the window and turned to face them.

"Come on then!" Kyle shouted, raising the bat once more.

Beside him, Lauren gripped the rolling pin, ready to fight, but she knew they didn't stand a chance. Just two of them couldn't kill this thing. It was too quick. Too strong.

Too dangerous.

5.40 p.m.

Kyle and Lauren stared at the creature that stood by the window and hissed at them.

"We have to attack together," Kyle said to his sister.

"Together," Lauren agreed.

But just as they raised their weapons, the front door burst inwards and a group of people bundled into the flat. They almost fell over each other as they pushed along the passage and came to a sudden stop when they saw what was happening.

Kyle and Lauren turned to see Nelson and two of his gang standing behind them in the living room. Nelson was holding a golf club, its end covered in brown gunk. There was more gunk in his black spiky hair and down the front of his leather jacket. The girl standing to his left was wearing torn jeans and a school blazer covered with studs and badges. She held a large table leg with a jagged end. Her Afro was spattered with gunk, and she had a wild look in her eyes. The boy on Nelson's right was JD, his tartan trousers and denim jacket streaked with muck. He gripped a baseball bat in both fists.

Nelson nodded once to Kyle, then looked at the creature and grinned.

"Right then, *freak*. Come get some," he said before rushing straight into battle.

Nelson's mates didn't hesitate to follow him. They screamed battle cries and rushed past Kyle and Lauren to attack the creature.

The creature screeched when Nelson hit it hard with the golf club, but he didn't stop. He hit it again

and again as his mates tackled it from either side, raining blows down on it.

The creature flailed its arms, trying to protect itself, but Nelson and his mates were relentless. They hit it over and over again until its legs buckled and it dropped to the floor.

"It's down!" Nelson shouted in triumph. "Get it! Before it disappears!"

They crowded around the monster, hitting it until brown gunk splattered onto the carpet and it finally lay still.

Nelson stood back, breathing heavily, and admired his handiwork.

"Not so tough now, are you?" he said, kicking the broken creature.

"We got it, didn't we?" said the girl who was with him. She had a streak of crusted brown gunk down one side of her face. "We got the sucker."

"Yeah, Trish, we got it," Nelson panted. "You all right, JD?"

The boy with the baseball bat looked up from the corpse of the monster and nodded. "Aye, man. I'm good."

Then Nelson turned to look at Kyle and said, "All right, Soldier Boy?"

"Um ... aye," Kyle replied. "You?"

Nelson raised his eyebrows and took a long deep breath. "Am I all right?" he asked. "Well, it's been a weird night. The building's full of freaky monster-things who want to suck our juices but ... Aye. I think I *am* all right."

"You're lucky we came in here," Trish said, flicking gunk off her broken table leg and looking Kyle up and down. "Otherwise, I reckon it would've sucked you dry." She glanced at Lauren. "Her too."

"We were doing all right," Lauren said, putting back her shoulders and standing as tall as she could.

Kyle watched his little sister, feeling proud. He didn't know where Lauren had suddenly found so much courage, but he was impressed.

"Aye, sure you were," JD said sarcastically. "Looked like you were goners to me. You need to get 'em down and get 'em quick; otherwise, they disappear and come back again somewhere else."

"I saw that," Kyle said.

"And you have to be careful of their spit," JD added, touching his face. "It burns like bleach or something."

Kyle noticed JD had red marks all over his face and thought he probably had the same. The creature had sprayed Kyle with spit and he had felt it burn, though the sting had faded now.

"Well, you don't have to thank us right now for saving you," Nelson bragged. "You can do that when we get out of here. You *do* want to get out of here, don't you? So just stick with us and—"

There was a "pop", and a creature appeared right in front of Nelson. It grabbed him with both claws, opened its mouth and clamped down on Nelson's neck.

Nelson screamed, then there was a "pop" and

the creature disappeared, taking Nelson with it.

5.48 p.m.

Everyone stood in shock and stared at the place where Nelson and the creature had been just moments ago.

"We have to get out of here." Trish was the first to break the silence "More of them will come. If one of them knows we're here, others will come."

"But ..." JD blinked hard. "It took Nelson. It just *took* him."

"We all saw it," Trish said. "But there's nothing we can do."

"We can get him back," JD argued. "I mean ... where did they go? They must go *somewhere*."

"Doesn't matter," Trish told him. "He's gone, and we have to get out of here. And I mean now."

JD turned on her with anger in his eyes. "That's our mate you're talking about. We *have* to try and save him."

"There's no point," Lauren said. "Once those things get you, that's it. Only thing we can do is try and get out of here. Like Trish said."

Kyle looked at his sister, feeling another burst of pride that she was being so strong.

"She's right," he told JD.

"Then maybe she should lead the way," said JD. He came so close to Kyle that the toes of their shoes were touching. "Maybe the little girl should be in charge if she's so clever," JD snarled.

"I'm right here." Lauren pushed JD away from her brother. "So if you want to say something, say it to my face. And I'm not a little girl."

The snarl fell away from JD's lips, replaced by a look of surprise. Then he frowned and straightened up so that he towered over Lauren. "Look, kid—"

"Keep your voice down." Trish grabbed JD's arm and pulled him back. "And leave them alone. You know she's right."

"They just stood there when that thing took

Nelson," JD snarled. "They didn't do nothing."

"You just stood there too," Trish said. "And me. It was too quick. Now let's get out of here before more come. That one's probably gone back to tell the others where there's food. And I don't want to be food, do *you*?"

Trish pushed past them and along the passage to the front door of the flat.

Kyle didn't like the idea of being food either, so he nudged Lauren and they followed.

"Looks clear," Trish said, looking into the corridor. "Stay close and think quick. If one of those things appears, hit it. Don't hesitate."

As she said it, the lights flickered and a series of popping sounds came from the living room.

"Now," Trish said, slipping out into the corridor.

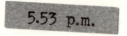
5.53 p.m.

They moved in single file, keeping close to the wall

as they crept along the dim corridor towards the stairwell. Trish, then Kyle and Lauren, then JD.

The ringing silence that had settled over Floor 5 of Alpine Heights was punctuated with dull thumps and muffled shouts.

The journey was agonisingly slow, but Trish was doing the right thing. Whatever those creatures were, they had good hearing as well as good vision, so the only way to escape was slowly and quietly.

They inched closer and closer until Trish finally stopped, a metre or so from the stairwell. She looked back at Kyle, shaking her head.

Kyle made a questioning expression: *What is it?*

Trish cupped her ear with one hand, then pointed at the door to the stairwell: *I hear something*, she mouthed.

Kyle heard it too.

Trish pointed at her chest, then at her eyes, then at the door, meaning: *I'm going to look.*

Kyle took a deep breath and nodded.

Trish crouched lower and edged towards the door. When she eased it open, Kyle saw over her shoulder into the stairwell.

Two creatures were on the stairs leading down to Floor 4. They still looked mostly human – their eyes hadn't yet become shining black orbs, but their skin was discoloured and lumpy, and their gaping mouths were lined with vicious teeth. One of them wore the remains of a black-and-white striped football shirt, and the other was draped in a torn hospital gown but wasn't Mrs Patel. They had their backs to the door and were fighting over something, pushing and screeching at each other. A third creature scuttled round the corner, climbing upstairs, then the light flickered and a fourth popped into view right beside them.

It was the strangest thing Kyle had ever seen. Stranger even than the creatures themselves. The light in the stairwell was bright enough for him to see it clearly: one moment there was nothing, and the next moment something materialised out of thin air.

The two creatures that were fighting turned in alarm, and Kyle saw what they were fighting over.

Another victim. A young man. The creatures each gripped him with their claws, like children fighting over a favourite toy.

Kyle leaned back, not wanting to see any more.

Trish did the same, closing the door quietly.

Kyle nudged her and pointed further along the corridor. He mouthed the word *Lift*.

Trish considered it, then nodded and moved on. When they reached the lift, she pressed the button and turned to make sure the others were behind her.

"The lift?" JD asked. "Is this a good idea?"

"Keep your voice down!" Trish whispered.

"Yeah," JD replied. "But the lift?"

"I agree," Lauren said, moving round so they were huddled in a group. "You're not supposed to use the lift in emergencies."

"That's for fires," Trish argued. "You can't use it if there's a *fire*."

Lauren and Trish both looked at Kyle, as if his was the final vote.

Kyle glanced along the corridor and shook his head.

"There's no other way down," he said.

"We could wait," Lauren suggested. "Find an empty flat and wait to be rescued."

"What if no one comes?" Trish said. "Or if those things find us first?"

"That's true," Kyle agreed. "And they found us just now, didn't they? I've been thinking about that and … well, what if they're searching all the flats, looking for … I dunno."

"Food," Trish said. "They're looking for food. And I already told you, I don't want to be food. Do you?" She looked at each of them in turn.

Obviously, no one wanted to be food.

"So we take the lift," Trish said.

"I'm not sure it's—" Lauren started to say, but there was a "pop" from behind them in the corridor, making her stop mid-sentence.

A few metres back, past the stairwell, dim white light shone from the flat they had just left. Beyond that, the corridor was in utter darkness. *That* was where the sound had come from.

The kids stayed silent, watching.

The hum of the lift grew louder as it approached.

Kyle pressed closer to the wall and squinted, wondering if he could see something moving in darkness. He couldn't be sure if—

Yes. There *was* movement. There, in the murky blackness at the end of the corridor. And when Lauren gasped, Kyle knew she could see it too.

"Oh flip," JD whispered.

A creature emerged into the shaft of dim light that spilled into the corridor. It stopped and turned its head like it was searching for a signal. And then it found something.

Kyle could tell the instant the creature noticed the rattle and hum of the approaching lift. Its entire body became focused. It seemed to be trying to work out what the sound was. Then it disappeared and reappeared much closer.

Trish pressed the lift button again, harder this time, as if it would make the lift come faster.

Kyle gripped his rounders bat and stayed close to the wall, trying to keep in the shadows. But the creature had locked on to the sound of the lift and was creeping closer. It was just a few metres away now. Any moment, it would spot the four kids huddled in the dark shadows by the lift.

"C'mon, c'mon, c'mon," Trish muttered, stabbing at the lift button again and again.

The lift cables rattled in the shaft, followed by a heavy clunk as the lift shuddered to a stop. Kyle gritted his teeth and kept his eyes on the creature as the door clattered open and bright light spilled into the corridor.

The kids were suddenly lit up like actors under a spotlight, and the creature saw them right away. It let out a high-pitched screech and began scuttling towards them.

5.56 p.m.

"Get in!" Trish shouted. She leaped into the lift and started hammering at the "close door" button as the others bundled in behind her.

Kyle pushed Lauren against the back wall of the lift. He stood in front of her, side by side with JD. But Lauren was determined to fight too. She squeezed between them, holding her rolling pin.

"Stay back," Kyle told her, but Lauren ignored him. She stood her ground, right beside her brother, ready to fight.

The lift door began to close.

Slowly.

Painfully.

Almost closed …

The creature appeared right in front of the lift, its gnarly arms reaching in. Kyle leaned away and swung his bat. There wasn't much room, and the bat passed just inches from JD's nose as it arced down to hit the creature's arms. The creature screamed, and Lauren stepped forwards to spear her rolling pin into its mouth. Trish smashed her broken table leg down on the nearest clawed hand.

The bony fingers snapped, and the hand pulled away, leaving a trail of brown gunk running down the edge of the door, but Trish didn't stop. She battered the other claw, forcing the creature to back away from the lift. Finally, the door clattered shut, and the lift whirred into life and began its journey downwards.

Kyle leaned against the gunk-streaked metal wall, out of breath from the battle.

"You OK?" he asked his sister.

Lauren nodded, then pointed to her brother's face. "Are *you*?"

Kyle touched a ragged cut on his cheek and looked at the blood on his fingers.

"You'll live," JD grumbled. "And well done, by the way. You two got more guts than I thought."

"It's not over yet," Trish said.

As if to confirm it, there was a loud bang on the roof, and the lift shuddered to a halt.

The kids looked at each other in alarm, then raised their eyes towards the ceiling.

"It's on top of us," Lauren whispered.

The lift suddenly lurched, throwing the kids off balance. Then there was a long groan of metal grinding against metal, followed by a terrifying twang of something snapping. Debris rained down inside the shaft, and then the whole lift dropped.

5.58 p.m.

Since moving to Alpine Heights, Kyle had used the lift more times than he could count. Sometimes, after stepping in, he had watched the door close and felt like he was in a giant metal coffin. He had stared at the "Maximum Load" label and wondered what would happen if the cables snapped and the lift dropped.

What would it feel like?

Would he survive?

He was about to find out.

Metal squealed against metal as the lift plummeted down the shaft.

Kyle's heels rose from the floor as he became weightless. His stomach heaved upwards, and he grabbed the handrail that ran around the inside of the lift. With his other hand, he reached out to Lauren, wanting to protect his sister. But there was nothing he could do. The lift gathered speed, falling faster and faster, the four occupants hurtling to their doom.

But almost as suddenly as it had started, the lift slammed to a sudden stop, throwing the kids to the floor in a painful heap.

Kyle was twisted uncomfortably, with Lauren lying across him. Trish was on her back in the corner with her legs up against the wall, and JD was curled into a ball with his butt in Kyle's face.

The metal coffin was filled with the sound of heavy breathing and the trickle of dust and dirt falling onto the roof.

"What the hell just happened?" JD mumbled.

"Emergency brakes maybe," Trish said, picking herself up. "Lucky. I thought we were dead for sure."

"Lori? You all right?" Kyle asked as Lauren climbed off him and got to her hands and knees. "Are you hurt?"

"I don't think so," Lauren replied. Her face was pale and streaked with dirt. Her eyes were bloodshot and had a distant look in them.

"We'll get out of here," Kyle told her. "I promise."

"How?" Trish challenged him. "We're trapped in a metal box at the bottom of a lift shaft. The doors are shut, if you hadn't noticed."

"Then we'll have to open them," Kyle said.

"And what if those things are out there?" Trish asked.

"Then we'll fight them," Kyle told her. "And we'll beat them. And we'll get out of this building." He stared at Trish. "You OK with that?"

Trish grinned. "Aye, Soldier Boy, I'm OK with that."

Without another word, Kyle picked up Trish's broken table leg and jammed the end into the small gap at the edge of the door. He levered it hard, forcing the door open until there was a gap big enough for him to get his fingers in.

"Feel free to help anytime," Kyle grunted as he tried to pull the door open with both hands.

JD moved forwards to help, then Lauren and Trish. They put all their strength into it, pulling the door until eventually it began to open, bit by bit.

"Oh bum, we're between floors," Trish said when the doors were open enough for them to see the concrete wall of the lift shaft.

"Not quite," Kyle told her. "Look up."

Just above head height, there was a gap with a faint light shining through.

"Give me a leg-up," Trish said. "I'll have a look."

Kyle laced his fingers together and held them out for Trish. She stepped on and reached for the lip of the concrete as Kyle pushed her upwards.

"It's the first floor," Trish whispered, peering over. "We've just missed it, but I reckon we can climb up. It looks clear." She heaved herself up and squeezed through the gap.

Her legs kicked a couple of times as she dragged herself out of the lift, then she was gone. A couple of seconds later, her face appeared in the gap.

"Come on," she whispered. "It's clear."

Kyle made a step with his hands again, expecting Lauren to climb up. Instead, JD pushed in front of her to use Kyle's step and drag himself out of the lift.

"Oh aye, very nice," Kyle said sarcastically. "Make

sure you're all right, why don't you?" Then he turned to Lauren. "Now you," he said. "Come on."

"Wait!" Trish hissed from above. "Someone's coming!"

Lauren paused with her foot on Kyle's hands. The two of them stared at each other, listening to the sound of movement in the corridor above them. Then there was a flickering of bright lights, and someone shouted, "Stay where you are! Don't move!"

"Please!" Trish called back. "Don't shoot. We're not infected."

Then came the sound of scuffling and more voices before bright torchlight pointed directly into the lift.

"You two in there," said a muffled voice. "Stand back so we can look at you."

"Wh-what?" Lauren replied, turning her face away from the bright light.

"Stand back now or we'll shoot!"

"Do what he says," Kyle told Lauren. He was remembering what they had seen from the window upstairs when they'd been hiding in the empty flat. He hoped the soldiers had been shooting the infected, but maybe they had just been shooting people trying to escape from the building.

Lauren stepped down, and they pressed themselves against the back wall of the lift.

Torchlight shone directly at them.

"They look all right," said the muffled voice.

"You sure?" came the reply.

"Not infected as far as I can tell."

There was a pause, then, "All right. Bring them out. We'll take them for processing."

The light pointed away, and a head appeared in the gap. It looked like one of the Special Forces soldiers who had been outside the building earlier. He was wearing a black helmet and had a gas mask covering his face.

"All right, kids," he said from behind the mask. "I need you to move forwards one at a time."

Kyle didn't hesitate to push Lauren forwards.

The torchlight focused on her, running up and down until the soldier said, "You're fine. Take my hands and we'll get you out of here."

Without waiting for an answer, the face disappeared and a pair of gloved hands came through the gap.

Lauren looked back at Kyle.

"Go on," Kyle said. "I'm right behind you."

She took the hands and let them pull her out of the lift.

As his sister's feet slipped out of sight, there was a series of pops in the corridor above.

"We have multiple targets incoming," said a muffled voice. "Approaching quickly."

"Engage! Engage!" said another voice.

Bursts of gunfire exploded in the corridor.

"Where are they coming from?!" a soldier yelled.

Between the gunshots and panicked voices there was the shrieking of creatures. Smoke and the acrid smell of gunfire filtered into the lift.

"They're everywhere!"

"Man down! Man down!" The shout was followed by a horrible scream that could only have come from a human being.

Still trapped in the lift, Kyle could only imagine what was happening. And he was imagining the worst.

"Lauren!" He had to get to her. He had to be with his sister. He had to look after her.

Frantic, he jumped up and grabbed the concrete edge of the first-floor corridor. His legs pedalled as he tried to gain traction to push himself up. He had to be strong enough. *He had to get out.*

"Keep firing!" someone shouted.

The shooting continued in rapid bursts. It was punctuated by shrieking and screaming and soldiers barking orders.

"Get the kids out of here!"

"There's one still in the lift!"

"Leave him. We need to retreat!"

It was almost deafening inside the lift, but Kyle

heard that last order clearly. It echoed in his head as flashes ignited in the dark and smoky air of the corridor.

Leave him.

No way. There was no way that was going to happen.

Kyle scrambled harder, getting one elbow onto the edge. He looked up and saw Lauren in the arms of a soldier who was backing away along the corridor towards the exit. From the other direction, creatures were appearing as the soldiers fired at them with automatic weapons. Some creatures went down, bullets ripping through them, spraying the walls with brown gunk. Others popped in and out of existence, moving closer and closer. The creatures grabbed soldiers and smashed through their gas masks before tearing at their faces.

"Kyle!" Lauren screamed, seeing her brother trying to climb out of the lift. "We have to help him!" She struggled to get free of the soldier holding her.

Kyle's elbow slipped, and he fell but quickly picked himself up again. He went to the back of the lift and took a short run up before jumping as high as he could. He grabbed the edge above him and used his momentum to pull himself up onto his elbows.

He was going to make it this time.

"Kyle!" Lauren yelled as she broke free of the soldier and rushed forwards. She threw herself down, skidding along the floor and grabbing the back of her brother's shirt to pull him out of the gap.

At that exact moment, Kyle heard a "pop" behind him and felt the lift move as it took on extra weight. Strong claws gripped his waist and began to drag him backwards.

"No!" Lauren screamed as she pulled harder on Kyle's shirt.

But she wasn't strong enough.

The shirt ripped out of her fingers, and Kyle disappeared into the lift.

There was a "pop", and he was gone.

REPORT: X5F812

TOP SECRET
___

Interview with: LAUREN DEMPSEY
Date: 4th November 2020

The following is taken from an interview with Lauren Dempsey, forty-three years after the incident at Alpine Heights.

___

LAUREN DEMPSEY: That was the last time I ever saw my brother alive. And even though that happened forty-three years ago, I still see his face in my dreams. I *still* see the fear in his eyes when he was pulled away. People don't believe, or don't want to believe, what happened that night, but it's true. All of it.

NIGHT HOUSE AGENT: Can you tell us what happened after that?

LAUREN DEMPSEY: After those things took my brother?

NIGHT HOUSE AGENT: Yes.

LAUREN DEMPSEY: The soldiers removed us from the building. Me, Trish and JD. They took us to a quarantine area that was basically a large military tent with some camp beds and a few medical supplies, but they had no idea what they were dealing with. Not right then, anyway. Someone checked me over, looked in my eyes, took my blood pressure, but I don't think she was even a proper doctor.

NIGHT HOUSE AGENT: Were there other survivors in the tent?

LAUREN DEMPSEY: Yes, there were. Trish and JD, and a few others. I couldn't tell you exact numbers, but not many. A handful at most. I didn't take much notice because I was numb. I'd been running on adrenaline up to then and had finally started to crash. The soldiers put us on a bus with blacked-out windows and made us sit apart – so we couldn't talk to each other, I assume. They took us to some kind of hospital and kept us apart there too. I was in a room about the size of a prison cell, with a bed and not much else. I think I was there for about three months, but that's a guess. They tested me, drugged me, gave me shock therapy. It's all a blur, but I think they were trying to make me forget. Which I did, mostly. It was when I started to see Kyle's face in my dreams that it all came back, piece by piece. Anyway, they eventually put me into the care system. Lucky for me, I had good foster parents who adopted me in the end … otherwise who knows where I'd be now.

NIGHT HOUSE AGENT: Did you ever see Trish or JD again?

LAUREN DEMPSEY: Well, as you know, I've been trying to find out the truth about Alpine Heights for most of my career. I've been discredited because of it. I've lost jobs and been threatened. As part of my search for the truth, I managed to track down Trish a few years ago – Patricia Adeyoye. She lived alone in a small flat in London. I visited her for an hour, and we talked about Alpine Heights, but she didn't remember much. When I went back the following day, she claimed she didn't know me. She said she had never lived anywhere called Alpine Heights. Someone got to her, of course. Probably threatened her or drugged her, I don't know. Anyway, she refused to speak to me again. JD on the other hand ... Well, I couldn't find anything about him at all. It's as if he never existed.

Article taken from Monthly Publication

THE CRONEAN TIMES, December 2020, ISSUE #189

Woman Disappears from Plane!

Greetings, readers! Well, I know how much you all love a creepy locked-room mystery, but this takes things to a whole new level. On 7th November this year, Lauren Dempsey, a lawyer from the United Kingdom, disappeared from a plane! Ms Dempsey boarded the British Airways Dreamliner 787 flight to Rio de Janeiro, along with 250 other passengers, but when the plane reached its destination, there was no sign of Ms Dempsey.

The passenger in the seat beside her claims that Ms Dempsey went to the toilet mid-flight but never returned to her seat. When completing pre-landing checks, airline staff noticed that the toilet door was locked, but when they entered it, the cubicle was empty. Ms Dempsey was not there. Upon landing, police searched the plane and found nothing but Ms Dempsey's hand luggage and her suit jacket.

But the mystery runs even deeper because Ms Dempsey was a survivor of the Alpine Heights disaster of 1977 (see issue #142) and fought endlessly to reveal the truth behind what happened that dreadful night. Hopefully we'll bring you more on this story next month.

> There were no further mentions of the incident in The Cronean Times, nor in any other publication.

NIGHT HOUSE FILE NUMBER ME347:
The Deadsoul Project

Author's Conclusion

The Night House investigation into what happened at Alpine Heights confirms that on the evening of Wednesday, 2nd February 1977, Lauren Dempsey, Trish Adeyoye and someone identified only as "JD" were taken to a secure facility and kept in quarantine for observation. An unknown number of other people from Alpine Heights were also transported to the secure facility. Those who displayed no symptoms of mutation were eventually released, while others were taken for more testing. The Night House couldn't find any evidence of what happened to Private Connor Fleming, but rumours suggest he was taken alive from the building.

The official government report said that what happened at Alpine Heights was caused by "Legionnaire's disease as a result of a contaminated water supply". Several residents died, and the building was isolated. Surviving residents were rehomed elsewhere and never allowed to return. The managing agent in charge of the building was quickly arrested and prosecuted for allowing the communal cold-water storage tanks to become infected with Legionnaire's disease. Relatives of those who died in the incident were each paid a large sum of money as compensation and signed an agreement to not take the matter any further. The building was condemned and remained unused until it was demolished on 7th August 2024.

An investigation by special agents from the Night House concluded that the event at Alpine Heights on Wednesday, 2nd February 1977 was nothing to do with Legionnaire's disease but was a direct result of top-secret Military Project TP731.

All evidence of the event was then covered up by Military Intelligence. Surviving residents were either paid off or threatened, or both, and there was a targeted campaign to discredit anyone who ever dared to speak out about what happened. None of the former residents of Alpine Heights ever spoke publicly about that night, apart from Ms Dempsey.

Lauren Dempsey went on to become a lawyer and searched for the truth about what happened in Alpine Heights. She worked tirelessly, despite efforts to discredit her. Eventually, she spoke to Night House agents about the incident, but three days after that interview, Lauren Dempsey disappeared in mysterious circumstances.

She boarded a plane to attend a conference in Rio de Janeiro, Brazil, but when the plane landed in Rio, she was not on it. She was missing, as if she had vanished into thin air. But she was definitely on that flight. She had checked in, her name was on the manifest – I have seen it myself – and her hand luggage was on board. The passenger in the seat next to hers claims that she went to the toilet mid-flight and never returned.

But how could she have disappeared from an aeroplane flying 30,000 feet in the air? I'll leave *you* to think about that. I'll also leave you to decide what to believe – was Legionnaire's disease to blame, or was it something else? Something much darker and more dangerous?

I don't know why the Nightwatchman chose to send me *this* file and ask me to write *this* particular story, but I have my suspicions. I believe that Project TP731 is ongoing, and that a similar anomalous event could occur at any time. I also have my suspicions about Lauren Dempsey's disappearance.

One thing is for sure – we must remain vigilant.

CLASSIFIED

THE WINTERMOOR LIGHTS

Coming soon ...

The truth no one wanted you to hear

THE WINTERMOOR LIGHTS
THE NIGHT HOUSE FILES

Dan Smith

Illustrated by Luke Brookes

TOP SECRET

THE WINTERMOOR LIGHTS

Released: September 2025

On Friday this week, a dozen children failed to turn up for lessons at Wintermoor Comprehensive School. After a police search, all of the missing children were found unharmed in different locations around Wintermoor. According to reports, the children were behaving strangely when found. They seemed to be in a trance, and several of them were muttering incoherently.

A teacher from Wintermoor Comprehensive who wishes to remain anonymous said: "It's some kind of prank. It has to be. Some of the children even claim to have seen 'lights' in the sky over Wintermoor …"